"Are you telli... my father?"

"Isn't that what y... a few weeks preg... Her mother's ang... had flipped a switch. "I had no idea at the time. I thought if people knew you were mixed race…"

No! Reeling, Jolene tried to speak, but her voice caught in her throat. The room receded. Everything she'd ever known to be true…

"Does…does Daddy know? Or maybe I shouldn't call him that any more?"

"Yes, he knows. He took the two of us in without batting an eye and he's loved you like you were his own."

Like you were his own. The words couldn't have hurt more if Margaret had stabbed her with them. Hands shaking, she stumbled towards the door.

She had no idea where she was going or what she'd do.

The only thing she knew was that life would never be the same again.

Her Secret Family

SHERRY LEWIS

MILLS & BOON
SuperROMANCE

First published in Great Britain 2007
Harlequin Mills & Boon Limited,
Eton House, 18-24 Paradise Road, Richmond, Surrey TW9 1SR

© Sherry Lewis 2006

ISBN: 978 0 263 85786 3

38-0607

Printed and bound in Spain
by Litografia Rosés S.A., Barcelona

Dear Reader,

From earliest childhood, most of us get our clues
about who we are from our families. We create our
own identity based on the way our parents, siblings
and grandparents look at us. Some of us come to
believe things about ourselves so deeply, we never
stop to question whether they're true or not. We
become the quiet one, the smart one, the shy one
or the silly one because that's what we've been told
we are.

Jolene Preston has accepted what she's been told
all her life. So when she stumbles across evidence
that the "truths" she has always accepted about
herself aren't true at all, it throws her into turmoil.

Her Secret Family is the story of Jolene's struggle
to discover who she is after all the comfortable
childhood labels are ripped away. It is also a story
about finding, recognising and keeping love when
it finds you. Along the way she meets Mason
Blackfox and his twelve-year-old daughter, Debra,
who are facing struggles of their own.

I've come to care a lot about all three of them. I
hope you will, too.

Sherry Lewis

PS I love to hear from readers. You can reach me
through my website at www.sherrylewisbooks.com
or by e-mail at sherry@sherrylewisbooks.com.

For Carol Peterson,
a hero in every sense of the word

Acknowledgements

With grateful thanks to the many members
of police and fire departments who have
answered my questions on gender bias in the
workplace with honesty and integrity, most
especially to Captain Bill Stoddard of the
South Ogden Fire Department.

To Choogie Kingfisher for his helpful answers
on clan lines and for directing me to places
where I could find more information on the
Cherokee people. *Wado.*

CHAPTER ONE

IT WAS FRIDAY NIGHT. Date night. For most women, that meant Manolo Blahniks, slinky dresses and fine dining. For Jolene Preston, it meant steel-toed boots, her trusty 9 mm Beretta and a cold hot dog wolfed down on her way to a stakeout in one of Tulsa's older neighborhoods. Just the way she liked it.

Her back against the cold brick wall of an abandoned store, she tried to see through the late-night shadows. Fifty yards away, a single light burned in a fenced-in yard, just bright enough for her to see people milling around.

"Hey, Jo-Jo. You in position yet?" Her partner's voice was little more than a breath in the earpiece she wore.

"I'm here," she whispered, "but it's black as pitch. I can't see much."

"Yeah? Well maybe you should have stayed out here and let me take the back."

Coming from anyone else that suggestion would have felt like a challenge, but from Ryan Fielding it just made her grin. She and Ryan had been working together since she transferred into the Special Investigations Division eighteen months earlier. He was a good cop and a decent guy—one of the few men in the department who didn't feel threatened by women on the force. Jolene inched around a stack of rotting cardboard boxes. "Forget it, old man. You'd hurt yourself trying to get through the obstacle course back here. I wouldn't want that on my conscience."

Ryan chuckled as she'd known he would. The five-year difference in their ages had been a running joke between them since the one-and-only time he tried to cushion her from a harsh situation. She'd accused him of gender bias. He'd denied it, claiming instead that he thought she was too young to handle the job. It was as close to an apology as she was likely to get. Afterward, they'd settled into a working relationship that suited both of them.

"Any sign of Zika or his boys at your end?"

Jolene took another look at the men

behind the warehouse. Two years ago, Raoul
Zika had moved into Tulsa and set up a drug
operation, which Tulsa's finest hadn't been
able to shut down. "There are a few of them
back here. Can't tell what they're doing yet.
How close are you?"

"I'm there now, but it's like a morgue out
front."

Gauging the distance between her position and the fence, Jolene whispered, "I'm
still about fifty yards away. Give me a few
minutes to get closer."

"What the hell have you been doing?
Your nails?"

"Yeah, well, you know me, always dolling
myself up." Jolene checked the ground in
front of her with one foot and moved carefully around a stack of old newspapers. "I
stopped off to do a little shopping at that
secondhand store on the corner."

"Figures. It's awfully quiet around here
tonight," Ryan said as she slid behind a
battered white van parked in back of Capriotti's Sandwich shop. "You think Big Red
gave us the wrong information?"

"I don't know." Jolene didn't trust Red,
but who did? He was a junkie who'd do

anything for a fix. "He sounded pretty sure that Zika would be moving the shipment tonight."

"Yeah, well, he might just have been playing us," Ryan said, voicing her own thoughts. "He'd give up his own mother if he thought it would save him."

Jolene started to agree, when she heard something. The response froze on her lips. "I think there's somebody back here," she said, dropping her voice. Clouds covered the moon and stars, making it hard to see, but she heard something again, and this time she identified it as someone talking.

"Come on." It sounded like a young male. "Just try it. What are you worried about? Your dad's never gonna know."

Kids? Here? *Now?*

A second person spoke, the voice high-pitched and feminine. "He *might* be able to tell. He'd probably see it in my eyes or something."

"If you're that worried," the boy said, "just hang with me for a few hours until you come back down again."

"He's not going to let me stay out late. He barely let me come to the party at all."

Smart father. Jolene tried to guess how far the kids were from Zika's operation, but the way noise echoed in the alley made it hard to judge. Wherever they were, they weren't far enough.

Jolene could almost see the case they'd been slowly building against Zika—late nights watching his operation, uncomfortable interviews and countless hours spent with the scum of the earth—swirling down the drain.

"So call and tell him you want to stay longer," the boy bargained. "You can talk him into it, can't you?"

"You don't know my dad."

Something or someone banged into metal and Jolene decided they must be near the Dumpster not far ahead.

"C'mon," the boy taunted. "Your old man can't be that smart." His voice dropped, and Jolene missed whatever he said next. Then she smelled the stench of burning marijuana.

Frustrated and angry, she searched the shadows for the telltale red glow that meant somebody was inhaling. Every time a kid lit up, swallowed a pill or used a needle, someone like Raoul Zika was responsible.

She ached to get him off the streets, but if he and his men were moving a drug shipment tonight, they'd be heavily armed, probably high and definitely edgy. Ignoring those kids would be reckless and irresponsible.

Biting back her disappointment, she spoke into the mouthpiece. "Hold on, Ryan. I've got a couple of kids back here."

"Say again?"

"Kids—smoking up, by the sounds of it. Two. Maybe more. Not very old, either. I need to get them out of here."

Ryan swore. "How close are they?"

"Too close to ignore. If something goes wrong, they'll be right in the line of fire."

"Well, get 'em out of there fast, before Zika and his boys figure out something's going on."

That might be easier said than done. A couple of kids with a joint weren't likely to lie down and give themselves up if they saw her. Wiping away a trickle of perspiration, Jolene stepped carefully around a recycling bin, but she wasn't careful enough. Her toe hit a loose board and the clatter echoed up and down the alleyway.

The kids froze, the red glow disappeared and one of them took off at a dead run toward Zika's warehouse.

Damn! Tossing a warning at the girl to stay where she was, Jolene set off after him. She raced full-out, but the kid had the advantage. Halfway down the alley, she rammed into a garbage can and crashed to one knee. As she hit the ground, she heard the rattle of chain link, which meant the boy had reached the fence surrounding Zika's warehouse.

Shouts from a couple of men went up as Jolene staggered to her feet again, and she knew their chances of catching Zika doing *anything* tonight had just gone up in smoke. Why couldn't the kid have run the other way?

"Jo?" Ryan's voice sounded urgent in her ear. "What's going on?"

"The kids heard me and one of them took off," she panted. "He went over the fence into Zika's turf."

"Dammit! Have Zika's men seen him?"

"He ran right into their arms." Jolene took a second to catch her breath, then muttered, "We might as well shut down and get out of here. There's no way Zika will move that shipment now."

"Eisley's not going to be happy," Ryan grumbled.

"Tell me about it." And he'd blame Jolene. He always did. Captain Eisley had been trying to get Jolene out of his previously all-male unit since the day she transferred in—but he flew just under the radar, making it impossible for her to prove.

As she turned back, pain shot through her leg and nearly knocked her off balance. Her palms burned where bits of dirt and gravel had embedded in her flesh, but none of that came close to matching the irritation she felt. He was a skinny kid, she *should* have been able to catch him.

To her surprise, the girl still hovered behind the recycling bin. Too high to know she was in trouble, or too frightened to move. Either way, Jolene planned on having a few words with her.

Brushing wind-tossed hair from her eyes, she radioed Ryan to let him know what was happening, then strode to where the girl was hiding. "Hey—are you all right?"

"M-me?"

"Yes, you. Why don't you come on out of there?"

"That's okay. I'm fine right here."

Jolene glanced toward the warehouse and moved in closer. "Well, I'm glad to know you're okay, but I really need you to come out where I can see you."

The girl hesitated then sidled out from behind the bin, eyes wide, one corner of her lip clamped in her teeth. She couldn't have been more than eleven or twelve—a mere wisp of a thing with wide eyes and long dark hair. "Am I in trouble?"

"Well, that depends. What are you doing out here at this time of night?"

The girl raised one thin shoulder. "I was at a party with some friends."

"Yeah. I saw the party you were having."

"Not that one!" Somehow, the girl's eyes grew even wider. She nodded toward the apartment building at the end of the alley. "My friend lives over there."

"Then what are you doing out here?"

"Just taking a walk."

"Yeah, me, too. Why don't we get out of this alley? You can tell me your name while we walk."

Those big wide eyes narrowed in a hurry. "Do I have to?"

"I'm afraid so."

"I don't want to get in trouble."

"It's a little late for that."

The girl shifted from one foot to the other, glanced at her only escape route, then lifted her chin defiantly. "You can't get me in trouble if you don't know who I am."

"You don't think so? You might be surprised what I can find out." When the girl didn't say anything, Jolene pushed a little harder. "Look, sweetheart, you have two choices. You can tell me yourself, or let me find out on my own. I'll be a lot happier if you just answer my questions."

The girl stared at her for a long moment, then let out a heavy sigh. "Okay. Fine. My name's Debra. Blackfox."

Blackfox, huh? Jolene could tell at a glance the girl wasn't full-blooded. "You just made a good decision, Debra Blackfox. Did you smoke the weed?"

"I don't have to tell you that."

"You'd rather have us run tests down at the station? Okay. That's fine with me. Now come on out of there."

Debra pulled back sharply. "Why? Are you going to arrest me?"

For what? Being too young, too naive, too trusting and too needy? None of those were crimes, although judging from the number of lives Jolene had seen ruined by the combination, they ought to be. She shrugged. "If you won't cooperate, I'll have to take you in for questioning."

Debra slowly sidled out from behind the Dumpster. "I never said I wasn't going to cooperate."

"Well, that's good." Aware of how much time had passed, Jolene took her arm and started walking. "So did you smoke the weed?"

"No."

Jolene couldn't see any obvious signs of intoxication, so maybe she'd interrupted in time. "Then that's your second good decision of the day. What's your friend's name?"

"I—I dunno. I just met him."

"Then what are you doing out here with him in the middle of the night?"

A blast of warm wind tousled the girl's hair. She brushed it from her cheek and frowned. "He wanted to take a walk."

And she'd been so flattered by the attention, she'd jumped at the chance. What *was* it with some girls? Their mothers ought to teach them not to be so needy, and somebody ought to care enough to keep them off the streets. "How old are you, Debra?"

"Sixteen."

Right, kid. And I'm Mother Theresa. "Sixteen, huh? Do you have your driver's license with you?"

"No, I—I left it at home."

Jolene was in no mood for lies and evasions. "Listen up, Debra. You and your friend just caused big problems for my partner and me. Understand? So now tell me, how old are you really?"

"Fourteen."

"You don't look fourteen."

"I look young for my age."

"Apparently. What happened to the joint?"

"What joint?"

"The one your friend was trying to get you to smoke. Did he drop it?"

"I don't know."

Jolene thought about going back to search for it, but decided to let it go. Even if she found it, she couldn't prove Debra had ever been in possession, and they already wasted too much time in the court system, prosecuting cases against the little guy while the real criminals went on about their business. "Where will I find your parents?" she asked.

"My *parents?* Why do you want them?"

"Because I'm not leaving you here alone and I'm not taking you back to that party. You're a minor, so that leaves just two choices—the police station and *then* your parents or straight home. Which would you prefer?"

"But you can't—" Debra broke off and wrapped her arms around herself. Tears pooled in her eyes, but Jolene couldn't tell if they were genuine or just very convenient. "Let me go back to my friend's house, please. I promise I'll stay there."

"I'd rather talk to your parents and make sure they know what's going on. Are they at home right now?"

Debra sniffed and shook her head. "I don't know where my mom is. I haven't seen her since New Year's."

That explained a lot, poor kid. "You must live with somebody. What about your dad? Is he around?"

Debra nodded miserably. "Yeah."

"You live with him?"

"Yeah, but we live way out on Riverside Drive. The Riverview Apartments. It's a long way from here."

Jolene ground to an abrupt halt. She had moved into the Riverview Apartments herself a month earlier, and the coincidence jarred her. She had no idea if Debra was telling the truth about where she lived. She'd spent more hours at work than at home, by a long shot, and she'd never even set eyes on her closest neighbors.

"Well, Debra, it looks like this is your lucky night. I live way out on Riverside Drive, too. Is your dad at home right now?"

Debra looked disappointed, but not worried. "I don't know. Maybe. He wanted me to spend the night at my friend's house, so I don't know what he's doing."

"If that were true," Jolene pointed out, "your friend wouldn't have been trying to talk you into calling him."

"I don't know where he is. He doesn't tell me where he's going."

Did Debra have a mother missing in action? An uncaring father? Had she lied to her boyfriend, or was she lying to Jolene now? Frankly, the world had too many absent and uncaring parents in it, and far too many kids running around wild as a result. Slimy as pushers and users were, they were still a few rungs higher on the ladder than negligent or abusive parents. Those people had no business even *having* kids.

They reached the end of the alley and Jolene steered Debra toward the car. Ryan stood on the sidewalk tall, fit, dressed in a black T-shirt, jeans and a black leather jacket so he could blend into the shadows. "Let's go see if your dad is home. Maybe I can even convince him to pay more attention to what you're doing."

Debra looked skeptical, but she fell into step. "Okay, but it's not going to matter what you say. He doesn't care what I do. You'll see."

Jerk. "Then we'll just see what I can do to change his mind." Jolene gave the girl what she hoped was a reassuring smile and led her around the corner.

Body language practically shouting "annoyed," Ryan strode toward them. "Who have we got here?"

"Debra Blackfox," Jolene said. "Claims to be fourteen."

Ryan ran a quick glance over Debra's face. "I doubt that. What are you going to do with her?"

"Take her home."

"We can drop her at the station on our way back," he said. "Let her folks come and get her."

The muscles in Debra's shoulders tensed and Jolene could almost feel her fear. "At this time of night? You know what kind of creeps are at the station now."

"She's hanging out on the streets and smoking pot," Ryan pointed out as he stepped off the curb toward the car. "I think she'll survive."

Jolene took Debra by the arm as they started across the road. "I never said she wouldn't survive. But she's a kid, and she wasn't the one holding. What would you want us to do if this were Chelsea?"

"If she were my kid?" Ryan glanced over his shoulder. "I'd want her to know she was in serious trouble."

"He wants to take me to jail?" Debra asked.

Jolene shook her head and kept walking. "Don't worry about it. Everything will be okay." She didn't speak again until she'd helped Debra into the backseat and shut the door. Keeping her voice low so the conversation wouldn't carry, she rounded the front of the car and leaned against the hood beside Ryan. "She's a kid," she repeated. "I think she's scared enough already."

"What are you doing, Jo? Getting all maternal on me?"

Jolene glared at him. "That's a stupid question."

"So what's the big deal? Let's just take her downtown and let the boys there call her parents. She'll be fine."

"We're twenty minutes from her subdivision. If you don't want to take the time, I'll drive her there on my way home. Apparently, we live in the same complex."

Ryan gave her a look, but he stopped arguing. "Fine. Whatever. Just don't let Eisley find out about this. You know what he'll say."

Jolene had a pretty good idea, but she wasn't getting personally involved in a case. If they didn't take Debra to the station, there wouldn't even *be* a case. Ryan slid in behind the wheel, and Jolene hurried to the passenger door.

She wasn't feeling maternal, she told herself again. She'd just been around long enough to know that behind every kid making a stupid decision, there was a parent making one first.

CHAPTER TWO

"No," MASON SAID for the third time in as many minutes. "Get somebody else to help you. I'm not interested."

He could see Ike over the half wall separating the kitchen from the dining area of his apartment, hands spread wide in a gesture intended to look helpless. "Fine. Just tell me who. I'm open to suggestions."

That oh-so-innocent expression didn't fool Mason for a second. He and Ike Dearman had been friends for over twenty-five years. He knew every trick up the other man's sleeve. "Give up now and save your breath. You know how I feel about all that stuff."

He might as well have been talking to the wall. "This isn't about the Center or about the tribe," Ike said. "I'm writing this article to honor Henry's memory. Are you going to tell me you have a problem with that?"

Mason pulled the last two plates from the dishwasher and shoved them into the cupboard. "No, I don't have a problem with that. I just don't want to be a part of it. I walked away from that life a long time ago. I'm not going back."

"Nobody's asking you to go back," Ike said. "I could talk to half a dozen people and get nowhere. Nobody knew Henry the way you did."

"Except you."

"Yeah, but I can't interview myself. How stupid would that sound? And I can't be expected to remember everything. That's why I need your help. The tribal elders want to pay tribute to Henry for all the work he did. Maybe you don't care about honoring Henry, but I do."

Mason had never been able to refuse Henry anything. Ike knew that. He was obviously counting on it to sway Mason's decision. It was a cheap shot, but not wholly unexpected.

For some reason which Mason had never clearly understood, Henry had opened his home and his heart after Mason's mother died. He'd had no reason to. They weren't related by blood. But they had been members of the same clan, and Henry had set great store in that. Maybe that should have warmed Mason to the lifestyle Henry embraced, but there were just too many other factors and too many memories working against it.

Ike had been a refugee at Henry's, too. The son of some distant relative whose mother had abandoned him to chase life in the white world. Ike had been living with the old man for a couple of years when Mason arrived, and he'd seemed so indescribably cool Mason had developed a case of hero worship that had lasted until he was out of high school.

He knew better now. Ike had good qualities and some not-so-good, just like anyone else, but they were still closer than most brothers. They also knew each other's hot buttons, and if the stakes were high enough, neither hesitated to push.

Mason put away the leftover chicken and pulled two bottles of water from the fridge. Tossing one to Ike, he said, "That was a low blow. You know I loved the old man."

"So help me with the article. Let me interview you."

Mason still wasn't ready to give in. Ike had always been more interested in Henry's lessons about the old ways than Mason, and he'd remained heavily involved in tribal affairs as an adult. Mason had turned his back on his heritage and the memories he'd never been able to outrun the minute he was old enough to start making his own decisions.

"I loved the old man, but I have no intention of rehashing all that stuff he crammed down our throats night and day."

Scowling, Ike cracked the seal on his water bottle. "That's one helluva way to look at it. All he ever did was teach us who we are and where we came from."

Yeah, but that was the problem. Even Ike didn't completely understand why Mason felt such revulsion when he thought about where he'd come from, or why he'd sooner jump off a cliff than go back.

He pulled a bag of chips from the top of the fridge and brought it into the living room. He shoved a box filled with Ike's research materials, sat on the couch and dug around for the remote. "The game is waiting."

"On Tivo. It's not going anywhere." Ike

nudged the box toward Mason and tried again. "My article is due in two weeks. Give me one hour. That's all I'll ask you for."

"Yeah, until next—" The sharp and unexpected peal of the doorbell cut him off.

"You expecting somebody?" Ike asked, frowning down at his watch.

Mason shook his head and got to his feet again. "If there's a God in heaven, it's Barbara come to drag you home. Just as well, I suppose. I need to pick Debra up from the party in an hour. We wouldn't even see half the game if we started now."

He flipped on the porch light and yanked open the door. Debra. Standing on the porch next to an attractive woman who looked very serious.

Before he could recover from his surprise, the woman had run a quick, assessing glance over him from head to toe. "Mr. Blackfox?"

"That's right. I was going to pick Debra up. Am I late?"

The woman ignored his question and turned back one edge of her blazer to reveal a badge on her waistband. "Sergeant Jolene Preston, Tulsa PD. Could I have a minute?"

Confused and suddenly nervous as hell,

Mason nodded and stepped away from the door. "Why? What's going on? Debra, are you okay?"

"I'm afraid Debra's in a bit of trouble," Sergeant Preston said before Debra could get a word out. She stepped into the apartment and followed Debra across the tiny landing and into the living room.

"What's going on?" Mason asked again, trailing them.

The cop glanced at Ike, watched Debra curl into one corner of the couch, then finally turned to Mason with a thin smile and narrow, watchful eyes. "I found Debra with a young man in the alley behind Capriotti's Sandwich Shop about an hour ago. The young man was in possession of a controlled substance."

Controlled substance? Was she serious? Mason realized she was waiting for a response, so he forced a few words out of his tight throat. "What kind of controlled substance?"

"Marijuana."

Mason's mouth went dry. Drugs? His daughter was hanging around with someone who had *drugs?* Was she out of her ever-loving mind? With her family history? He tried to read her expression, but she was too damn good at closing herself off. He couldn't tell if she was frightened, angry, sullen, resentful…or all of the above. "Is this true, Debra?"

His stubborn daughter didn't move a muscle. Didn't even look at him. But there was nothing unusual in that. Since moving in with him a few weeks earlier, she'd barely spoken to him. He didn't want to believe that a kid of his could do something so stupid.

He was dimly aware of Ike moving behind him, and the sudden silence as the TV went off.

"You were with someone who had drugs?" he asked. His voice sounded unnaturally loud, but he couldn't seem to control it. "Do you want to tell me just what in the hell you were thinking?"

Debra slammed him with a look that could have melted plastic.

The cop saw it and stepped between them. "If it helps at all, Debra was telling the boy no. She claims she didn't smoke anything, and I think she's telling the truth. I brought her home because she's young to be running wild."

"She wasn't running wild," Mason snapped. "At least she wasn't supposed to be."

Sergeant Preston went on as if he hadn't spoken. "Girls this age need parents to keep an eye on them. It's rough out there."

What was this? Parenting 101? Heaven knew, Mason needed it, but not like this. Not in the middle of his living room on a Friday night at the hands of the police. It brought back a whole slew of unwanted memories.

To make things even worse, Ike automatically stepped in. "He's a good father, Sergeant. He's just a little new at all of this."

Ignoring them both, Mason sat on the ottoman and tried to make eye contact with his unhappy daughter. What went on inside that head of hers? She was a kid. What did she know about drugs? He honestly didn't know whether to shout at her, hug her or shake some sense into her.

He decided to start with the basics. "Who were you with, Debra?"

"A friend."

"What's his name?" Ike demanded.

Debra dragged her gaze to Ike's chin and shook her head. "I don't know."

Much as Mason hated being lied to, he actually prayed that she was lying now. "Some friend. Where did you meet him?"

"Why does that matter?"

"It matters," Mason said. "Tell me where."

Debra rolled her eyes in exasperation. "Why are you getting so upset? It's not that big a deal."

Mason could feel the heat rush to his face, but he tried to keep his voice level so the cop wouldn't get any wrong ideas. "You were in some alley with a drug user at midnight, and you don't think that's a big deal?"

"It wasn't midnight, and I didn't *do* anything. You're acting like I did. Ike, tell him he's getting all upset for nothing."

This wasn't the first time in the past few weeks that Debra had tried cutting him off at the knees by running to Ike. He sent Ike a warning glance and looked Debra squarely in the eye. "This is between you and me. Don't drag Uncle Ike into it. Ike, thanks for your help, but Debra and I need to work this out on our own. I know you understand."

Whether he did or not, Ike nodded and

crossed to the door. "Whatever you say, little brother. I'll… uh…I'll leave my stuff here and get it from you tomorrow, okay?"

Ike and his article had just plunged way down Mason's priority list. He waved his agreement without looking up and a second later he heard the door close. Sergeant Preston stood to one side, arms folded, observing them without expression. It would have been easier to talk to Debra without her, but she didn't seem inclined to leave, and he wasn't about to ask her.

He rubbed his face with his palms, then leaned forward, resting his forearms on his knees. "Did you smoke the pot?"

She glared at him. "No."

"Were you planning to?"

"Maybe."

"For God's sake, why?"

"Just to try it, I guess. To see how it made me feel."

"You *guess?*" Too agitated to sit, Mason got to his feet. "Why in the hell would you want to do something like that?"

"Shouting at her isn't going to make things better," Sergeant Preston said, putting a restraining hand on his arm.

He took a step away from her. "Excuse me, Sergeant, but this isn't *your* twelve-year-old daughter calmly telling you she's thinking about becoming a drug addict."

"That's not what she said."

"Not in so many words."

"It might help if you'd remember that she didn't actually *do* anything."

"She's thinking about it. Doing it is the next step."

"It doesn't have to be, and I don't think frightening her is the answer, do you?"

Mason felt the slim hold on his temper slip. "Oh, great. Let's pat her on the head and tell her everything's okay. Is that your answer?"

Not a muscle in the Sergeant's expression moved, but something flickered in her eyes. "It might be good to calm down and recognize the positive things Debra did tonight."

"Just as soon as you explain why you think this is nothing to worry about."

"I didn't say it's nothing to worry about, Mr. Blackfox, but losing your temper certainly won't keep her from taking things a step further next time. Don't underestimate your influence on her."

"I'm not losing my temper," he assured her. "But if I had any influence on her, we wouldn't be having this conversation."

"I'm sure if you just talk to her—"

"Talk to her." The tension of the past few weeks, combined with a fear he could barely name, began to tighten in his shoulders. The years rolled away and he was six, standing in front of a police officer who had responded to a call from a neighbor. No amount of talking had made a difference then. He couldn't image what good it would do now.

"That's a great idea." He could hear the heavy sarcasm in his voice, but he was too irritated to care. "I'll have to try it some time. Meanwhile, I think *this* discussion is over."

The sergeant's eyes flashed and her mouth opened, but Debra cut her off before she could speak. "Stop it."

Mason clamped his mouth shut and turned to see which of them she was talking to. Not surprisingly, she seemed upset with him. He just couldn't figure out why. "Stop what?"

"You're being rude."

"*I'm* being rude?" Was she even listening?

Debra scrambled to her feet and glared at him, her fists clenched tightly and planted on her narrow hips. She looked so much like his mother, the resemblance terrified him. "You're just mad because Jolene's right. You're a horrible dad, and I wish I didn't have to live here."

Mason shut down his fear and hurt, and concentrated on the anger. It was easier to deal with. "Yeah? Well I'm sorry you feel that way, but tough luck, kid. You're stuck with me for now."

"Not if she takes me away from you."

"Who? Your mother? I wouldn't hold my breath if I were you." Debra flinched and Mason realized how callous that had sounded. He backtracked quickly. "If your mom had her way, you wouldn't even be here," he assured his daughter. "Whatever the problem is between you and Bill—"

"The only problem *I* have," she shouted, "is *you!*" And with that, she bolted down the hall and slammed her door so hard the front windows rattled.

JOLENE WATCHED the emotions play across Mason Blackfox's face while a whole different set of emotions ran through her. She was embarrassed for him, not to mention surprised that he seemed so concerned about his daughter. The way Debra had talked, Jolene had expected to find something completely different. Mason was articulate and intelligent and, yes, sober.

She hadn't expected that.

She hadn't expected him to be so tall, either. So broad-shouldered. So good-looking in an outdoorsy way she didn't usually respond to. His dark hair was combed neatly away from his face, trimmed so that it barely grazed the back of his neck. Well-defined muscles stretched a black T-shirt with a faded logo across his shoulders and chest. Jolene would have bet a week's paycheck he hadn't built them at any gym. But what caught and held her attention was a long, narrow scar running along his jawline. She couldn't help wondering when and where he'd received the injury that had caused the scarring—and how.

"Mr. Blackfox—"

"Would you leave, please?" He spoke without looking at her.

Maybe she should leave. Ryan certainly

would. Who was she kidding? Ryan wouldn't be here in the first place. But Jolene had never liked turning her back on someone who was hurting, and it was obvious that Mason Blackfox was in pain. So was his daughter. On top of that, they were her neighbors. How could she just turn her back and walk out the door when they might bump into each other tomorrow at the mailbox or by the pool?

"I'm sorry," she said. "This must be difficult."

Very slowly, Mason turned to face her. "You don't need to worry about me losing my temper and hurting my daughter, so feel free to go."

"I'm not worried about that," she assured him. "How long ago did her mother leave?"

He scowled. "What does Debra's mother have to do with this?"

"I just thought Debra might be having trouble adjusting to her mother being gone."

His lips curved slightly. "I see. Well, Sergeant, I don't think that's the trouble."

"Jolene," she said. "I live over on the other side of the complex. I don't see any reason to be formal since we're neighbors."

Mason processed that too slowly for comfort. Just when she began to wonder if she'd offended him, he went on. "Debra's mother left me nine years ago and took Debra with her. They've been living together in Kansas City all this time. Debra's only been back in Tulsa for about eight weeks."

Jolene's next comment died on her lips. "But she said…"

Mason's smile grew a fraction of an inch. "Apparently, she said her mother abandoned her."

Had she? Jolene couldn't remember. That was certainly the impression she'd gotten, but was it what Debra said?

"Well, she didn't. Her mother is still living in Kansas City and she works for one of the major newspapers there. She's a respectable woman with a respectable job and a brand-new respectable husband. Debra is living with me because she doesn't like it there."

What *had* the girl said? Jolene had asked if her mother was home, and she'd said… She'd said she didn't know where her mother was. That was it. Jolene had assumed the rest.

Her cheeks grew warm and the back of

her neck burned. "I must've misunderstood what she meant."

"I'm sure she meant for you to misunderstand," Mason said. "Debra's my daughter, and I love her, but she never does anything without a reason, and she's not the easiest kid on the planet to live with. She's got an attitude, and she knows how to use it."

"It's pretty obvious Debra feels abandoned by her mother."

Mason sank onto the couch and tossed the remote onto the coffee table. "What are you, some kind of psychiatrist?"

"No, but—"

"So you don't really know what you're talking about."

"I've had plenty of experience with people, Mr. Blackfox. Debra's perception of her circumstances has a powerful influence on her behavior."

"I'll keep that in mind. Now if you'll excuse me, I have things to do." He glanced pointedly at the door. "Can you find your way out—?"

Jolene pulled out a business card and jotted her direct line and cell numbers on the back. "Unfortunately, drugs are readily available. Kids have them, and they know where to get them."

"My kid shouldn't."

"But your kid does." She tossed him the card. "If you hear her mention the name of the boy she was with, let me know. You might also want to look into some community service programs for teens. Sometimes another adult can get through where a parent can't."

An expression of distaste crossed his face.

Jolene stood and reached across the coffee table to hand him the card. "No promises, but we'll do what we can."

As anxious to get out as he was to get rid of her, Jolene turned abruptly and rammed into the coffee table, knocking a box filled with documents. Mason let out a shout and dived for them, but it was too late. Jolene watched as what must have been a thousand pieces of paper fluttered to the floor.

CHAPTER THREE

MORTIFIED by her clumsiness, Jolene knelt to help him gather loose papers. "I can't believe I did that. Look at the mess I've made."

"It's fine," he said, but his voice had a razor-sharp edge to it. "Leave it."

"I'm the one who knocked it over," she argued.

A scowl dragged at the corners of his mouth, but he took the small stack of documents she handed him. "It's not mine. It's Ike's," he said, dumping them onto the coffee table in a heap. The top layer began to slide toward the floor, but Mason didn't seem to notice.

Jolene caught the sliding stack, leveled it and reached for the box at her feet. "Did he have all of this in any particular order?"

"It doesn't matter," Mason said. "He can fix it tomorrow."

Jolene ran a doubtful glance over what looked like hundred of pages of research and pictures. "My dad's a history professor at the university, and he spends most of his time researching. I know how important it is to have everything where you can find it."

"Ike won't care," Mason assured her. "I doubt it was in any particular order, anyway." He reached past her for a stray document.

Jolene's gaze was inadvertently drawn to the muscles in his shoulders. "What is he researching? Something about the Cherokee, it looks like."

"He's writing an article about the founding of the Cherokee Cultural Center."

"I know the place," she said. "It's on the north end of town, isn't it?" At Mason's nod, she said, "I've never actually been there, but I've driven past it a hundred times."

"You and the rest of Tulsa." Mason started a new stack on the coffee table, but he took more care this time to make sure they didn't topple. "The Center's thirtieth anniversary is coming up in a few months. The man who raised us was one of the founders, so the elders asked Ike to write something for the tribal newspaper."

"So you're Cherokee then?"

Mason retrieved some photographs from under the table. "I am."

Jolene knew people of Native American descent, of course. You couldn't grow up in a place like Tulsa without meeting them. But her parents had never encouraged those friendships when she was young, and she was embarrassed to admit that her circle had widened only marginally as an adult.

She sat back on her heels with a handful of newspaper articles, curious to see what kind of research Ike had pulled together. The top article was a story about a donation of land to the Western Cherokee. She skimmed it briefly and flipped to the next picture of a group of people in front of a familiar adobe building.

Though the Center was larger now, Jolene had no trouble recognizing the landscape and the original facade, but the people were another story. A man of about forty stood smiling in the center of the photograph with a taller, much younger man beside him. But it was the woman next to him who captured Jolene's attention. If she hadn't known better, she'd have sworn she was looking at a picture of her own mother.

She glanced up at Mason. "This is an interesting picture. Was it taken at the Center's opening?"

Reluctantly, he leaned in close to take a look. "It was."

Jolene could smell his aftershave and the faded scent of garlic from dinner. "And the people in the photograph? Who are they?"

"Does it matter?"

"No. I'm just curious." A trait that served her well at work, but didn't always endear her to people in her private life.

Mason shrugged and pointed to the central figure. "That's Henry Owle. He's the man who raised me." He moved his finger to the tall good-looking man with the confident smile. "And that's Billy Starr. He died in Vietnam shortly after this picture was taken."

"And the blond woman?"

"Margaret Starr. Billy's wife. She wasn't Cherokee, but Henry told me she was very involved in getting the Center opened."

"Her name was Margaret?" What an odd coincidence. "Is still alive?"

Mason shrugged again. "I wouldn't know."

There certainly was a remarkable resemblance between the two Margarets. More than remarkable, actually. The similarities were so strong, it felt almost spooky. The woman in that photograph was a dead ringer for her mother.

Slowly, she became aware of Mason watching her, a frown on his face, and the apartment suddenly felt way too small and *way* too stuffy. She handed him the articles and stood.

"Something wrong?" Mason asked.

Jolene shook her head. "No, I'm just tired. It's been a long day."

With a quick goodbye, she hurried down the stairs. She thought she heard him say something, but she didn't stop to find out. In the parking lot, she let herself into her 4Runner, and immediately the sense of urgency vanished.

Confused, she leaned her head against the back of her seat and closed her eyes. She wasn't sure what happened to her in there, but she didn't like it.

"FIELDING. PRESTON. In my office. Now!"

Jolene glanced up from her computer screen to find Captain Eisley in the open doorway, red-faced and breathing heavily. He was built like a bulldog, all chest and round face, with narrow hips and short, squat legs. He was probably in his late forties, and the years had etched lines around his mouth and into his forehead.

She met Ryan's gaze across the space separating their desks, clicked to save the report she'd been working on and stood. Ryan jerked his head toward Eisley's office, and she followed, dreading the next few minutes.

Anything that got Eisley worked up like that was a bad thing. The fact that it had something to do with them made it even worse.

Mike Santini, one of the longtime members of the unit, grinned as she passed him, obviously delighted to think she might be on the hot seat. Jolene pretended not to notice. Mike had strong opinions about women on the force, and he never hesitated to share those opinions, even when no one else wanted to hear them. He was loud, brash and abrasive—more brawn than brains—and one of the worst practical jokers in the unit.

So far, he'd left Jolene alone, but that was just because he didn't like her well enough to target her. If ever she found a pizza delivery sticker pasted to the side of her 4Runner or her desk in the men's bathroom, she would know she'd arrived.

Ryan made it to Eisley's glassed-in office first and claimed the good plastic chair for himself, which left the one with the short front leg for Jolene. *Jerk.*

Captain Eisley shut the door behind them—not a good sign. It didn't matter all that much, anyway. The two large plate-glass windows that looked out over the bull pen meant that every man out there could watch what happened next.

Clearly angry, the captain launched his attack before Jolene even had all her weight in the chair. "Would one of you mind telling me what the hell happened last night?"

Jolene tried to position her feet so the chair wouldn't tilt every time she moved. "We had to abort the operation, Captain. I found a couple of kids in the alley."

"So you just let Zika waltz off with a heroin shipment?"

"No, sir. One of the kids took off running. I tried to intercept him, but he reached the fence around Zika's warehouse before I could. Once Zika's men saw him, it was too late."

Eisley sat behind his desk, where a half-eaten dried-out sandwich lay forgotten on top of a paper bag. The scowl on his face strengthened his unfortunate resemblance to a bulldog. "Some kid outran you? How did that happen?"

Jolene would have given anything for a better answer. "I tripped."

"You tripped?"

"Could have happened to anybody," Ryan said in her defense.

"I was in an alley," Jolene said. "And it was dark. There was garbage all over the place."

Eisley waved off her explanation and linked his stubby fingers over his stomach. "This isn't about you tripping, Jolene. This is about the fact that you took your eye off the ball. You were there to follow through on a lead. If you hadn't been distracted, we might have gotten what we needed to put Zika away for a long time."

The hair on the back of her neck stood up and a low warning buzzed inside her head.

"There were kids in that alley, Captain. I thought they were in danger."

"They weren't in danger until you sent one of them running straight into Zika's camp."

Ryan cleared his throat. "We don't know that—"

This time Jolene waved him off. She couldn't afford to have the captain think she needed help fighting her battles. Back rigid, she sat forward. The chair tilted onto its short leg with a *thunk*. "I did not put those children in danger, Captain. The danger already existed. If Ryan had made a move and those men were armed—"

"That's a hypothetical situation, Jolene. Yes, that might have happened, and yes, if all the stars lined up just right, the scenario might have played out the way you thought." Eisley shook his head and set his chins jiggling. "But the point is, we'll never know what might have happened. All we can go on now are the facts. The fact that you put that boy in danger by trying to roust him."

The buzz in her head grew louder and Jolene could've sworn she could feel the hair on her arms growing. He was going somewhere with this, but she wasn't sure she wanted to know where. She forced herself to ask, "What are you saying, Captain?"

"I'm saying that there's no room on this team for that kind of thoughtless action. We've talked about this before, Jolene. You know my rules. It's all about the team."

She couldn't believe they were even having this conversation. Not after last night. The whole thing felt surreal. She heard Ryan take a breath and knew he was getting ready to defend her again. The chair tilted back again, so she stood. "The team would have taken a direct hit with the media if anything had happened to those kids, and you know it."

Eisley's cold blue eyes hardened. "We're not talking about what might have happened in some fantasy you dreamed up out there last night. We're talking about reality. The reality is, you're still not focused and last night proves it. We were closer to nailing Raoul Zika than we've ever been, but we lost him. We may never get that close again."

"Big Red got us the information once," Ryan said. "He can do it again."

"If he's willing to talk."

"He'll talk," Jolene assured him. "He made a deal with us to drop that possession charge in exchange for information. He'll do almost anything to avoid going back to lockup."

"Including ratting out Raoul Zika twice?" Captain Eisley laughed without humor. "We were lucky he opened his mouth once."

"Then we'll just have to make sure he does it again." Ryan got to his feet and stood beside Jolene. "I was there last night, Captain. I know what happened. Jolene did nothing wrong."

"Loyalty is commendable," Eisley said. "Just make sure you're putting yours in the right place." He sat back in his chair so he could glare at both of them. "Now get out of here and see if you can find Big Red again. Maybe you can still pull this out of the fire."

Seething, Jolene was halfway out the door when Eisley called after her. "Preston?"

Her stomach knotted into a hard lump as she turned back. "Yes, Captain?"

"You'd better pray Big Red comes through for you."

"Yes, Captain."

"Blow another operation like the one last

night, and I'll have no choice but to transfer you into some other less demanding unit."

As she had a thousand times since being assigned to Eisley's command, Jolene swallowed her pride and choked back everything she would like to say in response. Eisley might have won this round, but if he thought he'd won the war, he couldn't have been more wrong.

CHAPTER FOUR

SHORTLY AFTER NOON on Sunday, Jolene parked in front of her parents' two-story brick house. After her discussion with Eisley the day before, this was the last place she wanted to be, but she couldn't very well cancel now. The every-third-weekend routine had been a cherished tradition of her mother's since Jolene's younger brother, Trevor, graduated from high school and Margaret officially became an empty nester.

Vowing not to say a word to her parents about this latest dustup at work, Jolene reached into the backseat for the bag of goodies she'd picked up on the way. Trevor's truck wasn't in the driveway—she'd arrived ahead of him for once. Maybe she'd earn a few bonus points this weekend.

Not that she and Trevor were in competition or anything. It wasn't like *that*. But

Trevor did have that annoying habit of doing everything right. He'd chosen the right career, dated the right girls, wore the right clothes and said all the right things. He'd even been accepted at Johns Hopkins, which had sent their history professor dad over the moon when Trevor broke the news last month.

Jolene, on the other hand, never quite felt she measured up. Oh, nobody *said* anything, but there were the looks her parents exchanged when she talked about work. The helpful suggestions her mother offered about visits to the cosmetic counter or some great sale on clothes Jolene would never wear. They tried to understand her choice of career and her driving need to make the world a better, safer place, but they just didn't get it.

Too bad Jolene couldn't explain it.

She'd never known what drew her to handcuffs instead of harmonic ratios and interrogations rather than the study of feudal indenture. She only knew she would never be happy doing anything else.

Popping the CD she'd been listening to out of the stereo, she tugged her duffel bag from the backseat and hurried up the sidewalk. At the door, she took a steadying breath, pasted on a smile and knocked once before letting herself inside. "Hey! Where is everybody?"

Her mother, the brilliant mathematician, appeared in the doorway at the back of the foyer, her pale hair gleaming, her face and makeup as fresh as if she'd started the day only a few minutes earlier. Jolene had spent a lifetime wishing she'd inherited even a fraction of her mother's charm. For all the good wishes did.

Jolene consoled herself with the knowledge that she was her father's daughter—intense, dedicated and single-minded.

"You're here," her mother said. "And right on time. I was afraid something would come up to make you late again."

Jolene winced. Eisley's ultimatum had left her edgy. She had to keep that in its own compartment. This was family time. She left her duffel bag by the stairs and carried the groceries into the kitchen. "Where's Dad?"

"In his study. Shall I call him?"

"Not if he's busy."

Making a noise with tongue and teeth,

Margaret waved away her objection. "He's just researching. You know how he gets."

Grinning, Jolene tossed her purse and keys onto the table. "Don't disturb him, Mom. He'll leave the cave when he's ready."

A frown creased the bridge of Margaret's nose, but she nodded and returned to whatever she was doing on the stove, Jolene following. "I suppose you're right. So, how is work?"

Jolene sat at the table. "Work's fine. How's life at the university?"

Her mother gave an absentminded nod. "Fine. Same as always, I guess." She glanced up and brushed hair from her forehead with the back of her hand. "Did you get a chance to call Rachel Brennan back?"

How long had she been here? Ten seconds? Twenty? Jolene slumped back and turned the crystal salt shaker in her fingers. That had to be some kind of record, even for her mother. For two solid weeks she'd managed not to think about the luncheon being planned by a few of the girls she'd known in high school, but she hadn't even been in her mother's house for two minutes before the subject was on the table.

"No, I've been busy."

"But you *are* going?"

"Probably not." Jolene tried not to sound defensive. "We're shorthanded at work, Mom. We have been for months now. Getting time away is next to impossible."

Margaret rolled her eyes. "Oh, but surely you can take an hour. They have to give you a lunch break. And you need to go. Those women are your friends."

"They're acquaintances, Mom. Acquaintances I haven't seen in more than ten years."

"Which is exactly why you need to catch up."

Propping her feet on an empty chair, Jolene wished she could find a way to avoid this never-ending conversation without hurting her mother. "I have nothing in common with any of them, and I have no desire to stand around Rachel Brennan's dining room pretending to care about what they've been doing."

The crease above her mother's nose deepened. "That's antisocial, Jolene. That's exactly the kind of attitude that makes me worry about you."

Ashamed at how quickly she could grow

exasperated with her mother, Jolene let her head fall backward. "It's *not* antisocial," she said to the ceiling, "it's self-preservation."

"It wouldn't hurt you to have a few friends."

"I have friends."

"I mean friends *outside* the department. You should go out. Meet friends for dinner. Take in a movie with girlfriends. *Date*."

Mason Blackfox's image flashed through her mind, but that only annoyed her more. Jolene met her mother's hopeful gaze. "I date."

"When?"

"*I date*."

"And the last time you went out with a man was—?"

"I don't know! I don't keep track."

Dropping her feet to the floor, she plowed her fingers into her hair. "Why do we have to talk about this every time we see each other?"

"I want you to be happy. I want you to have a full, rich life instead of one that's so lopsided."

"I like lopsided."

"Apparently. But that doesn't mean it's a healthy way to live."

"Mom, please—"

"Hear me out, Jolene, please. Every time I try to discuss this with you—"

"I'm not like you, part June Cleaver and part Sandra Day O'Connor. I can't do it all."

"Nobody can do it *all*, Jolene, and that's not what I'm saying anyway. But shutting yourself away from everyone and everything that doesn't fit into one compartment isn't good for you."

Jolene was too agitated to sit. "I'm going to take my things upstairs."

"Do you see what I mean? You're doing it again." Her mother came around the counter toward her. "What are you so afraid of, sweetheart?"

"I'm not afraid. I'm annoyed. There's a difference."

"With me."

Jolene couldn't bring herself to say yes. "With the situation, Mom. That's all. It just amazes me that you of all people have this old-fashioned idea about a woman needing a man to be happy."

"Oh, honey, that's not what I mean. Trying to get through life on your own the way you do… Well, you just make everything way too hard on yourself." Her mother tilted her head, and the expression on her face brought back the newspaper photo Jolene had seen at Mason's house. Funny that two people could look so much alike, and not quite fair that some stranger should bear such a striking resemblance to her mother when Jolene's own resemblance was so weak.

Desperate for a change of subject, Jolene said the first thing that popped into her head. "I saw something the other day that made me think of you."

"Oh? And what was that?"

"A newspaper article. I swear, there was a picture of a woman who looked just like you."

Her mother pulled a bag of tortilla chips from the cupboard and tore it open. "Oh, surely not *exactly* like me."

"Maybe not exactly, but awfully close. She even had the same first name. It was a surreal moment."

Her mother pulled hot sauce from the cupboard and filled a bowl. "Margaret isn't exactly an uncommon name."

"No, but it still caught me by surprise," Jolene agreed as she moved a stack of mail from the table. "One minute I'm talking to this guy about his daughter, and the next thing you know I'm looking at a woman who could be you. You weren't by any chance at the opening ceremonies for the Cherokee Cultural Center about thirty years ago, were you?"

A loud crash cut off her laugh and brought her around the counter. Pale and trembling, her mother stood over the shattered serving dish. Jolene grabbed the broom from the closet.

Her mother dragged her gaze up from the floor and touched one hand to her cheek. "I—I don't know what happened."

"It's okay, Mom. Accidents happen." Jolene bent to sweep glass fragments and chips into the dustpan. "I'm sorry about the dish, but I have to admit that it makes me feel better to know that you're human, too."

Still obviously stunned, Margaret pulled her hand away from her cheek. "That's quite a thing to say. Of course I'm human."

"I didn't mean to offend you," Jolene assured her quickly. "It was a joke."

"Well it wasn't funny." Margaret stepped over the shards of glass but chips crunched underfoot and her foot slipped a little in the hot sauce.

She caught her balance, but looked so lost and confused, Jolene abandoned the broom and stood to face her. "Are you all right?"

"I'm just tired. I didn't sleep well last night and I have a headache."

"Do you need some aspirin?"

"No." Her mother looked down at her hands as if they belonged to a stranger. "I think maybe I should lie down for a little while."

"I'll help you upstairs. "Jolene reached for her mother's arm.

Margaret jerked away and shook her head firmly. "No. I'll just… I'll be in my study."

Dumbfounded, Jolene watched her mother disappear down the hallway. She stood without moving, clutching the broom in both hands, until she heard the door close. Then, because she didn't know what else to do, she slowly bent back to the task.

Her mother had seemed fine when Jolene first came in. She'd even seemed okay after their argument. She'd seemed perfectly all right, in fact, until the moment Jolene asked about that photograph.

But why had *that* upset her?

Jolene wouldn't call her mother prejudiced, but she *had* always distanced herself from the Native American culture in Tulsa. Theirs was probably the only house within two hundred miles without a single piece of native art. But surely her mother hadn't reacted like that because of one teasing comment.

No, there was definitely something else going on here.

Determined to figure it out, Jolene pulled two bottles of water from the fridge and carried them to her mother's study. A chill traced her spine as she approached the door, and Jolene imagined she could feel her mother's negative energy trying to turn her away.

This wasn't the first time she'd imagined something like that, but these days she kept her impressions to herself. An overactive imagination, her mother had always said. Trevor had teased her mercilessly when they were younger, and Ryan thought she was two sandwiches short of a picnic for even suggesting she could feel another person's energy.

But she could feel something today, something so real it felt as if she'd walked into a pocket of hot humid air. She knocked softly on the door. "Mom? Can I come in?"

A long silence. She knocked again, louder this time. "Mom? I'm worried about you. Let me in—please."

Her mother finally opened the door and let Jolene inside. When she resumed her seat behind the desk she sat still as a stone, her fingers unmoving, her mind obviously a million miles away.

Jolene put a bottle on the desk in front of her. "What's wrong, Mom?"

Margaret's head snapped up. Instead of the reassuring smile Jolene hoped for, her mother's face paled. "Nothing. I'm fine."

"I don't believe you. You're not acting like yourself."

Margaret smoothed a hand across an open file folder and Jolene didn't miss the slight trembling of her fingers. "I've been having trouble sleeping, that's all."

Jolene moved a stack of books from a chair. "You were fine when I got here," she said, sitting. "Was it something I said?"

Margaret laughed sharply. "Honestly, Jolene, what an imagination you have. I'm tired, that's all. It's nothing to worry about."

"That's why you broke your favorite serving dish?"

Margaret frowned. "I dropped the dish because my fingers were still wet. It was an accident, nothing more."

"But—"

"But nothing!" Her mother's voice came out sharp and taut with tension, at odds with the careful smile she wore. "Really! This is too much. I said I was tired, and that's all there is to it. Let's not make a huge deal out of one clumsy mistake."

The rebuke was unlike her mother. "I know you're hiding something from me. The only thing I don't understand is why. We don't keep secrets in this family, Mom."

Margaret snatched up a file folder and tossed it into a stacking tray. "I will not have you treating me like a suspect in one of your cases, Jolene. I simply will not have it." Standing abruptly, she began shoving folders into the drawers of her credenza. "Is it too much to ask for a little privacy once in a while? Space to think? Do I really need to share every thought that goes through my head with you?"

Margaret kept her hands busy. "Honestly, Jolene, I don't know why you're making such a big deal about some old picture."

Jolene caught her breath. "I wouldn't make a big deal out of it," she said cautiously, "if you'd just tell me why it bothers you so much."

"It doesn't bother me. Everyone has a double—at least that's what they say."

"But it wasn't your double, was it? It was *you* in that newspaper article."

Margaret briefly glanced up from the file in her hand. "I don't even remember. It was all such a long time ago."

Jolene had spent too many years on the police force not to recognize a bald-faced lie when she heard one. "How did you become involved in the Cherokee Cultural Center?"

"Does it really matter?"

"Apparently it does."

"Do you tell *me* everything that happens in your life?"

"I think I'd explain something like this if you asked."

"Like what? Some old, silly picture in the newspaper?"

"An old, silly picture that claims you were

married to some stranger just a few months before I was born. Yes. I do believe I'd explain it to you if our situations were reversed."

Her mother turned away.

"Who is Billy Starr, Mom? Were you his wife?"

Margaret gripped the back of a chair and held on tightly. When she spoke, her voice was a whisper. "Yes."

Jolene had thought she was prepared for the answer, but it nearly buckled her knees. "Why didn't you ever tell me?"

"Because I didn't want you to know."

"But *why?*"

"It was a very brief period in my life. We spent less than a year together before they shipped him off to Vietnam, and he was only there a few weeks when he was killed in action." Margaret rubbed her arms. "He was one of the last men killed in that horrible war. I guess that was supposed to make me feel better. I don't know what it was supposed to do for you."

Jolene recoiled sharply. "For me?"

Margaret's eyes, filled with misery, met hers. "Surely you've figured it out."

Bile rose in Jolene's throat as a new, ugly truth rose up in front of her. "Are you telling me that Billy Starr is my father?"

"Isn't that what you want to know?"

No! Reeling, Jolene tried to speak, but her voice caught in her throat. It seemed to take forever to get it out. "*Billy Starr* is my father?"

Margaret's anger disappeared as if someone had flipped a switch. "I was only a few weeks pregnant when he shipped out. I didn't know at the time."

The room receded. Everything Jolene had ever known to be true… Her hands shaking, she stumbled to the door.

"Jolene! Wait!"

"I have to get out of here."

"No!" Margaret shoved past her daughter and stood between her and the doorknob. "He was a good man, Jolene, but he was gone and I was young. My parents were upset that I'd fallen in love with someone who wasn't…like me. I hadn't seen them in nearly two years because…because of the marriage. But I needed them. I was twenty-two and a widow. I had no idea what to do or how to get on with my life."

Jolene stared her down. "So they made you lie to me?"

"They didn't know. I thought if people knew you were mixed race... I wanted you to have every advantage."

It was too much to absorb all at once. "You wanted me to have every advantage but the truth," she said.

"Does...Daddy know? Or maybe I shouldn't call him that anymore. Does *Lawrence* know? Or did you lie to him, too?" The stricken look on her mother's face brought one brief twinge of regret, but Jolene's shock and outrage were far stronger.

"Yes, he knows. He married me before you were born. He took the two of us in without even batting an eye, and he's loved you like you were his own."

She was dimly aware of her brother standing in the middle of the kitchen, as she gently moved her mother aside and let herself out.

She had no idea where she was going or what she'd do when she got there. The only thing she knew for certain was that her life was never going to be the same.

CHAPTER FIVE

"BAD NEWS, CHIEF. Those phlox you ordered? Not here yet."

Chief? Mason looked up from the landscape plans he'd been reviewing. Doug, he thought the guy's name was. A new member of his crew. Had he meant that the way it sounded?

Doug couldn't have been more than twenty, and he didn't look especially bright, but he'd been working hard. The sweat-damp hair and stains forming under his armpits were proof of that. He waited for Mason's response with barely concealed impatience, shifting from one foot to the other and chomping on a piece of gum, but his broad face seemed open and his expression honest.

Mason shrugged off the potential racial slur. He'd been in a foul mood since Friday night. "The name's Mason," he grumbled. "Use it."

Doug lifted one bony shoulder as if to say *whatever*. "So what do you want us to do?"

Good question. "Who did you talk to at the nursery?"

Doug shifted the gum to the other side of his mouth. "I dunno. Some guy."

"You didn't get a name?"

"Didn't know I needed one."

"Always get a name," Mason said, his voice tense. "Then we know who to call again." He ran a hand across the back of his neck and tried to decide what to do now.

When the county commissioners voted to replace the landscaping around the complex several months earlier using a technique called xeriscaping, Mason had eagerly bid on the job. It was a huge, high-profile job ripping out the lawn and other high-maintenance ornamentals, and replacing them with drought-resistant plants native to the area. If the job went well, Mason's business would get a much-needed shot in the arm. If it tanked...

In spite of countless hours of planning, they were already more than a week behind schedule. Mason couldn't afford to lose more time. He'd worked too hard to climb out of the pit his parents had left him in. He wasn't going to go back without a fight. "Did they at least tell you when the shipment will be here?"

Doug gave another shrug. "Couple of weeks." He jerked his head toward the rest of the crew, waiting for Mason's answer. "Schweppe said to tell you. Wanted me to find out what you want him to do."

Mason rolled up the plans and slid a rubber band over one end. "Try Johnson Valley nursery. Ask for Antonio. Explain the problem to him and see if he can help us."

With a nod, Doug ambled off and Mason glanced at his watch. Just under three hours before the crew finished for the day. Enough time to start digging up the lawn on the north side of the complex.

He tossed the plans into the cab of his truck, filled Schweppe in on the change of plans, then, calculating that Debra should be home from diving practice by now, punched in his home number.

Things had been rocky between them for days. In fact, she'd given him the silent treatment for most of the weekend. He didn't know what she thought that would accomplish. She might not understand why the thought of her coming anywhere *near* drugs made him a little crazy, but that didn't mean he was going to change his mind about her Friday-night escapade or back off on the consequences.

The phone rang three times. Four. Five. By the sixth ring, Mason realized that Debra hadn't taken him seriously when he said she was to come straight home after practice. No stops along the way, no diversions. He had his finger on the off button when he heard Debra's sleepy voice. "Hello?"

Sleeping? At three-thirty in the afternoon? Mason warned himself not to jump to conclusions. She might have fallen asleep after school. "You sound tired."

"I just woke up."

"From a nap?"

"No."

"You were sleeping this late?"

Debra yawned. Stretched. "What time is it?"

"You haven't been up all day? Does that mean you missed an entire day of school and diving practice?

"I didn't feel good. I decided to stay home."

"You should have called me."

"I didn't want to interrupt you at work."

Mason kneaded the bridge of his nose. "Did you call Coach?"

"No. I was asleep." She yawned again, "You're mad at me, aren't you?"

Mason didn't have a clue which of the emotions climbing the walls of his stomach was the strongest. "I'm disappointed," he said, wincing a little as the word left his mouth. He'd hated when Henry used that word on him. It felt so manipulative. "Coach isn't going to be happy," he said, brushing past the guilt Debra was supposed to feel in response. "He went out on a limb adding you to the team in the middle of the year."

"It's only one practice. I'm not going to be here next year anyway, so who cares?"

"I care. The rest of the team cares. You should, too."

"I'll go tomorrow."

"Yeah, you will."

Debra must have moved into the bathroom because he could hear running water. "You don't believe me, do you?"

"That you were sick?" Mason shut the door of the truck and started down the hill toward the crew. "I'd sure like to, but lately I don't know what to believe."

"Because of Friday night?"

"That has something to do with it."

"I've already told you everything."

Mason put some more distance between himself and the crew. "You haven't even come close, kid. And there's still no TV or radio until I think I have the whole story."

Silence stretched between them.

"I didn't know he had a joint with him until I got outside."

Half a football field away, Schweppe tossed a couple of rakes into the back of a truck and turned to Mason expectantly. Mason waved for them to go on without him. "When you found out he had a joint, why didn't you walk away?"

"Because I didn't want to look stupid."

How many times had he heard that excuse in his lifetime? *I didn't want to be rude... They would have thought I didn't like them... I was only trying to be friendly.*

He gripped the phone tightly and closed his eyes. "This guy was trying to talk you into doing something not only harmful, but illegal. Why did you care what he thought?"

"Because. You just don't get it, do you?"

"Better than you might think. Walking away wouldn't have made you look stupid, Debra. Staying there and letting some jerk shove drugs at you looks stupid. You also broke your word to me. You promised to stay at the party. That's why I let you go."

"I just went outside to talk."

"And got picked up by the cops." Mason wiped sweat from his forehead with his sleeve. "You're lucky you didn't end up in worse trouble."

"I didn't *do* anything."

"You did plenty, Debra. You were with a kid in possession of narcotics. You were thinking about trying the drug. Don't you know how dangerous that could be?"

"It was just a little weed."

Mason's stomach twisted into a tight, painful knot. "Maybe you don't think it's a big deal, but I know better. People start out with 'just a little weed,' and end up addicted all the time."

"And people don't end up addicted all the time, too."

But not people like us. Mason wondered if telling her about his parents would make a difference, but why subject her to that kind of humiliation unnecessarily? Why subject himself to the memories?

"We'll finish talking about this later," he said. "And just so you know, I asked Barbara to drop by and make sure you're okay. She should be there any minute, so you can go ahead and open the door if you're sure it's her."

The water shut off and Debra's voice rose. "Are you kidding me?"

"No, why?"

"You're sending her to spy on me?"

"I'll feel better if she stops by."

"Why? Because you think I stayed home so I could lay around in bed all day and get high? I'm not that stupid, Dad. No matter what you think."

"I didn't say you were stupid, Debra. I just don't want to see you ruin your life!"

Something fell to the floor and shattered. "I don't need to ruin my life," Debra shouted. "You're already doing that for me." Three rapid beeps signaled a broken connection.

Mason punched the numbers in again, but

the phone rang straight through to voice mail. *Not cool, Debra.* Frustrated beyond words, he stuffed the phone into his pocket. Maybe he'd feel better if he worked himself into oblivion. Leaving work so he could drive home and yell at her wouldn't accomplish anything anyway.

A steady throbbing pain started in the back of his head and pulsed down his neck with every heartbeat. Barbara would be there soon. If there was anything to worry about, she'd let him know.

MASON'S HEADACHE was no better by dinnertime. In fact, it felt a whole lot worse thanks to the loud music coming from Debra's bedroom. Doing his best to ignore the heavy bass beat, he pulled a bag of salad out of the refrigerator and tore it open too roughly. Pieces of lettuce spilled onto the counter and the floor, and his frustration spiked.

He fisted his hands and planted them on the countertop, closed his eyes and counted to ten…three times. It didn't help.

She'd taken one look at him when he walked in the door, marched into her room with her nose in the air, and shut her door on him as he was midsentence. Nothing made Mason crazier than being ignored, and it had taken everything he had not to take her door off its hinges. Something his old man would've done.

At least Barbara had phoned him shortly after five o'clock and assured him that Debra had been home when she arrived. Alone. And that she'd seemed clearheaded.

His gaze strayed to the far side of the living room and the hallway that led to the small apartment's two bedrooms. This was normal teenage behavior, he told himself. All kids spent time in their rooms with the door shut.

He took three deep breaths and let them out slowly. Dinner, he reminded himself, and turned to the stove to check the leftover stew he'd put on the burner a few minutes earlier.

As he lobbed the empty salad package toward the garbage can, he realized that the trash was in danger of overflowing. He bent to pull a fresh liner from under the sink just as the phone rang, bringing him up too fast—straight into an overhead cupboard he'd left partway open.

Pain split his head and buckled his knees. He swore, slammed the cupboard shut and grabbed the cordless on the fourth ring. *"What?"*

"Hello to you, too. I was hoping to catch you in good spirits. I'm so glad to know my timing was right."

After nine years of only occasional phone conversations with his ex-wife, Mason was having as much trouble getting used to talking with her on a regular basis as he was to having a twelve-year-old in the next room. He rubbed his head gingerly and leaned into the corner of the cupboard. "Hello, Alex."

"You sound rushed. Did I catch you at a bad time?"

"No," he lied, "this is fine. I was just fixing dinner."

She laughed, and he imagined her curled in a chair with her feet tucked under her, her glasses pushed up on top of her head. "Lucky Debra. Does she appreciate all the effort you go to?"

When they were first married, Alexandra

had teased him for being so determined to put balanced meals on the table, but she'd gladly relinquished the role of cook. Later, when things began to fall apart, that teasing had turned bitter and she'd taunted him for the last year they were together about what she called his obsession with creating a "perfect" family.

Perfection had nothing to do with it. All he wanted was functional.

"I don't know," he admitted. "She doesn't say—to me, anyway. Has she said anything to you?"

"Not much, but she's still upset with me so that's not surprising. I tried calling this afternoon after school, but she wasn't home."

"She wasn't answering," Mason said as he swept up the lettuce on the floor. "She's not all that happy with me, either."

"Any special reason? Or was she in one of those moods she gets into because the sky is blue?"

Should he tell her about Debra's brush with the authorities? Probably. But some instinct warned him to keep his mouth shut until he knew more. If there was real danger of Debra using drugs, Alex would need to know, but he decided not to say anything until he had all the facts.

"We had a difference of opinion," he said, hoping a vague answer would satisfy her. "She didn't want to hear any more about my opinion, so she ignored the phone all afternoon."

"Isn't that just like her? Honestly, Mason, she used to be so sweet and easy to deal with—and then she turned twelve. It's like she became someone else entirely."

"You also decided to get remarried," Mason reminded her.

Alex's voice took on an edge. "And Bill's a terrific guy. He adores Debra. He's bent over backward trying to help her adjust to the changes in our lives. She's just determined not to adjust. How do you deal with a person like that?"

"I don't know, but I don't think that deciding she's trouble and shipping her off somewhere else to live is the answer."

"Well it's not as if I just put her on a plane and left her to fend for herself," Alex snapped. "I sent her to live with her father. Is she getting in your way?"

"That's not it at all." Mason dumped the

lettuce into the garbage bag and leaned the broom against the counter. "I love having Debra. It's what I've always wanted. But she's not happy here. She wants to go home."

"Don't you think I want that, too? Do you think I like this situation?"

"You could change it anytime you want."

"And lose my husband in the process." Alex's sigh was heavy with exasperation. "I know you think I'm being a horrible mother, and I understand why you feel that way. But try to see things from my perspective. I finally meet a wonderful man who is everything I ever wanted—no offense intended—and my daughter turns into some unrecognizable creature because of it. Am I supposed to let her ruin my marriage?"

"Are you sure she doesn't have cause for her reaction?"

"If you're implying there's something wrong with Bill, stop right there. He's done absolutely nothing to deserve the way Debra's been treating him. You're there with her. You see how impossible she can be. So please don't judge me. Just give me this time to put a new life together."

When Mason didn't respond immediately, she changed the subject. "Did Debra tell you about the report she has to do in her history class?"

It took a second for him to process the shift. "What report is that?"

"She's supposed to interview her grandparents, but I'm not sure why. She mentioned it to me last time I talked to her."

"I don't think she's said anything to me about it."

"You might want to check with the school to see when it's due. She's fallen into the habit of forgetting little things like term papers and tests lately."

"I can do that. I'll have her call your parents and talk to them while I'm home so I can make sure she actually does it."

"Yeah. Well, that's the thing, Mason. She doesn't want to talk to my parents. She wants to talk to yours."

"Mine?" He let out a disbelieving laugh. "My mother is dead and the old man is only God knows where. How does she think she's going to interview them?"

"I don't know. She told me she'd talked to her teacher and they'd figured out an alternative but she didn't go into detail. I thought you should know—considering how you feel and all."

An uncomfortable sensation churned in his stomach. "She can't do a report on my parents."

"She can, you just don't want her to."

"You're right about that!"

Alex's voice grew almost kind. "She feels bad because she doesn't know anything about them, Mason. She asked me why you never talk about them."

"You know why."

"Yes, I do. But she doesn't."

Were they really having this conversation? Only Ike knew more than Alex about his childhood and why Mason felt the way he did about his parents. She knew the damage they'd done and how hard Mason had worked to reclaim his life as an adult. "No, Alexandra. The less Debra knows about them, the better."

"I'm not so sure, Mason. Whatever their faults, they were her grandparents."

"Yeah, and I've lived with their legacy for thirty-five years. Trust me, that's not something Debra needs to be saddled with."

"I know how you feel about them," Alex

said. "I *do*. And I'm not saying you don't have good reason to feel that way. But you have to remember that Debra isn't you. She's never going to have to live with their neglect. It's an entirely different thing for her than it was for you."

"No! Don't encourage her, Alex, because it's not going to happen. If she needs to write a report on her grandparents, she can call your folks. You can think I'm the worst father on earth if you want to, but that's my final word. Now, I'm sure you didn't call just to argue with me. I'll call Debra to the phone."

"No. Wait. There's something else. It's important."

There was more? Mason ground his teeth together so hard his jaw popped. "So talk."

"I know Debra wants to come home," she said, "and I'm not insensitive to that. But Bill just took on a major client and trial is scheduled for the middle of October. It's a huge case. There'll be all sorts of work for him to do to get ready, and he's desperately concerned about not doing the job right if he's surrounded by distractions. I think— we both think that it would be better if Debra stayed with you for another six months at least. Until the trial is over, anyway."

Six months? Debra would have a fit. And who could blame her? "What are you doing, Alex? Letting Bill's career come before Debra?"

"I'm supporting my husband, and don't sound so smug. It's not as if you've never put your career first. That's one of the reasons I left, remember?"

"But this isn't about me, and it isn't about you, either." And it *sure* wasn't about Bill. "How are you going to explain this to Debra? She already thinks you've chosen Bill over her."

"I haven't," she snapped. "Bill and I are leaving town for a few days, and I might not get a chance to call again until Sunday. Tell Debra what's going on. I don't want her to be surprised by this."

"You want *me* to tell her? No way, Alex. You can deliver your own bad news."

"I thought you just said this wasn't about you."

"It's not. But you're not being fair to Debra. She feels—"

"I *know* how Debra feels," Alex said, her

voice crisp. "She doesn't exactly hide her feelings. But Bill's future hinges on this case, and he can't function at his best if he's fighting Debra all the time."

It had been a long day. A long *few* days, in fact. Things had gone wrong from the minute Ike walked through the door carrying that damn box of his. Mason's head hurt, his stomach ached and his nerves had been rubbed raw. "Who can?" he snarled. "You know what I think Bill's problem is?"

"No, but I'm sure you'll tell me."

"He doesn't have kids of his own. He doesn't get it."

"And you do?" Alex laughed. "If you think a couple of months at the head of the table makes you some kind of expert on raising children—"

"I know what it feels like to barely rate a notice from your mother. I know what it feels like to be less important than whatever man happens to be in her bed." He regretted the cheap shots instantly, but it was too late.

"You're a bastard, Mason. You don't have any right to lecture me, and you have no reason to compare me to your mother."

"You're right. I'm sorry."

"I've devoted every minute of the past twelve years to raising Debra, so stop trying to make me into some kind of monster because I found a man who actually loves me and treats me the way I want to be treated."

"I said I'm sorry, Alex. I didn't mean that."

When she spoke again her voice had lost its severity. "I should know how you get whenever the subject of your family comes up. After all this time I should know better than to even mention them. But I'm tired of watching you torture yourself, and I don't want you to start doing the same thing with Debra. I want her to get to know you while she's there, and I want her to get to know more about herself. For her sake, I hope you can put the past aside long enough to let that happen."

To make sure she got the last word, Alexandra disconnected just as Debra had earlier. Seething, Mason jabbed the off button and tossed the phone onto the counter. He *had* let go of the past. That was the whole point.

He'd buried it all—his parents, his childhood, the old insecurities and doubts. So why did everybody suddenly want him to dig it back up?

CHAPTER SIX

TWO HOURS LATER, Mason lugged the heavy garbage bag down the outside stairs on his way to the trash barrels behind the clubhouse. Dinner had been a disaster from the moment he'd dished up the burned stew to the second Debra had closed herself in her room and turned up the stereo again. From the first dirty look to the last hateful glare. You'd think he'd be used to it by now, but every one of Debra's sullen looks cut him.

He'd deliberated over whether to tell Debra about her mother's decision to leave her here, but they'd both been feeling so foul by then, he decided to leave it alone for the time being. He was going to have to tell her, though, and soon. The longer he put it off, the harder it was going to be.

He shifted the bag from one hand to the other and followed the sidewalk to the corner. Not that long ago, his nights had been taken up with late hours at work and an occasional night out. Now, he got excited by the prospect of hauling garbage, just so he could get a few minutes away from Debra's stereo.

There was definitely something wrong with this picture.

Being outside on a cool spring night had exactly the effect he'd hoped for, and within a few minutes his head began to clear. As he trudged across the long stretch of grass, one of the things Henry had taught him as a child ran through his mind.

Each morning upon rising, and each evening before sleeping, give thanks for the life within you and for all good things the Creator has given you.

Easier said than done, Henry.

Give thanks for all the opportunities to grow a little each day. Consider your thoughts and actions of the past day and seek courage and strength to be a better person. Seek for the things that will benefit others.

Well, let's see. In the past few days, his daughter had been dragged home by the police, Ike had stirred up the past, he'd become even further behind on the county complex project and his ex-wife had told him to disappoint their unhappy daughter again. There were probably plenty of opportunities for growth there. It was the being thankful part he got hung up on.

Lost in thought, he stepped off the curb just as a dark 4Runner roared around the corner. When he realized it was heading straight toward him, he jumped back onto the grass a split second before the vehicle rushed past, so close he could feel the heat from its engine.

He glared after it, trying to memorize the license plate. To his delight, the thing screeched to a halt and the driver's door opened.

Okay. Bring it on. He had a few things to say to the idiot behind the wheel, and he was in just the frame of mind to say them.

"Mr. Blackfox?"

The sound of a woman's voice surprised him almost as much as hearing his name. He was even more surprised when the pretty cop from the other night clambered out of the 4Runner, leaving the engine running and the door hanging open.

The last time he saw her, she'd worn her

hair pulled back from her face. Now it hung loose to her shoulders, soft and dark and shimmering in the streetlight. She wore frayed jeans, tennis shoes and a pale green sweater that hugged her curves in a way her blazer hadn't.

"I'm so sorry," she said, smelling faintly of something fruity. "I didn't see you. Are you all right?"

She looked so distraught, he bit back a sarcastic response and nodded. "I'm fine. You were going a little fast for inside the complex, weren't you?"

She glanced behind her at the 4Runner, as if it had done something outside her control. "I…Yes, I…" She brushed her hair away from her cheek and he noticed that her eyes seemed a little wild, and her fingers were trembling. "Look, I'm really sorry. I'm just glad you're all right."

"No harm done. What about you? You seem shaken. Is something wrong?"

"I nearly ran into you."

He held up the garbage bag, "Don't let it bother you too much. I had my handy safety bag to cushion the impact."

"You carry that around all the time?"

"Pretty much. It's the latest thing in personal safety. Haven't you heard?"

She shook her head but watched him cautiously, as if she couldn't decide how to take him. "I'm afraid I haven't."

"Well, you know what they say—the cops are always the last to know." Propping the bag at his feet, he said, "I never did thank you for bringing Debra home the other night. It was beyond the call of duty, I'm sure."

Jolene looked back at the 4Runner, as if now that she knew he was okay, she was eager to be on her way.

Too bad. After the day he'd had, Mason could think of worse ways to spend a few minutes than talking to a beautiful woman.

"It wasn't out of my way, and I wasn't going to leave her at the station. She's a little young for that. How's she doing?"

"She's sullen and angry. Barely spoke to me over the weekend. Slept most of today, missed diving practice and barely spoke to me at dinner. Things are pretty much normal."

A half laugh escaped Jolene, which seemed to surprise her. "It's really that bad?"

"She's just an unhappy kid, and I'm not sure I know how to help her with that."

"It's easy to tell that you love her."

"Well if that's enough, then I'm in good shape." It felt so good to be talking to someone who wasn't wishing he would crawl into a hole and disappear, he almost didn't want the moment to end. But for all he knew, she had a husband and kids waiting at home.

"Sorry for flinging myself at your car that way. I'm glad there was no damage. I'll let you get on home to your family."

She stiffened slightly. "My family?"

"I thought maybe you were hurrying to get dinner home to the kids or something."

Her expression cleared. "No, I'm not married. No kids, either."

"That's surprising."

"Why?"

"I don't know. A woman who looks like you…" He left the rest unsaid. No sense making a complete fool of himself.

"Thank you, but I don't think looks have very much to do with marriage."

"Just not interested?"

She looked surprised by the question. "Most men are put off by what I do. Guys tend to shy away from a woman who can cut them off at the knees and then slap on a pair of handcuffs."

"Well, that's their loss." Again, she smiled, but her gaze flicked to the 4Runner once more and this time Mason took the hint. "I don't want to keep you. Just wanted to say thanks."

"I'm being rude. I'm sorry. I'm just distracted."

"Is something wrong?"

She had to think about that for a second, but she shook her head as she slipped her fingers into the pockets of her jeans. "No. Well…sort of, but it's personal. You know."

Yeah, he did. Still, he felt compelled to ask, "Anything you want to talk about?"

She took a step backward. "No, but thanks."

"Anytime."

She walked away and Mason told himself to do the same, but like a kid at the pet store, he stood on the curb and watched as she climbed behind the wheel and shut the door between them.

JOLENE SLEPT FITFULLY that night. She hadn't had a good night's sleep since her mother dropped the bombshell. She dragged herself out of bed just as the sun came up and went out for a run that lasted until her lungs felt ready to burst and the muscles in her legs burned. Usually she could count on physical exercise to help her think through problems and gain perspective. Today even that failed her.

Her mother's story ran relentlessly through her mind accompanied by images that flashed in and out as if they were on a tape loop: her mother standing in front of the Cherokee Cultural Center; her father—*Lawrence*—the way he looked in their wedding picture; Billy Starr smiling as if an entire lifetime stretched out in front of him. Even Mason Blackfox, though she had no idea why he should keep popping into her head. Except that knocking over that box at his house was what started this whole thing.

She stopped at the Burger King on the corner, grabbed French toast strips and a large coffee, and walked back to her apartment, trying to decide how to fill the next few hours. She didn't have to be on shift until eleven o'clock, and the last thing she wanted to do was spend the time thinking.

As she rounded the corner of the building

next to hers, the sight of her mother's BMW parked behind the 4Runner brought her to a stop. Of all the nerve. Furious, she started walking again, this time straight for the driver's side of the car.

"What do you think you're doing?"

The window came down and her mother's face appeared, eyes red-rimmed and deeply shadowed.

"I need to talk to you, Jolene."

"There's nothing you can say I want to hear right now." Jolene turned away, fully intending to go inside and let her mother sit out here and stew. It was childish, she knew, but Margaret had called the shots for thirty years and Jolene needed to feel some control.

It didn't matter anyway, because her mother kept talking as if she'd agreed to listen. "I've been just sick since I told you about Billy," she said as she got out of the car. "And I know how upset you've been. But you can't go on being this angry with me. We need to resolve this."

"How do you propose to resolve it, Mom? Are you going to turn back the clock? Undo the past? Are you going to tell me it was all just a dream? That Dad really is my father, and that neither of you has been lying to me for the past thirty years?"

Her mother locked the car using her key chain remote, apparently planning to stay for a while. "Your father and I should have told you the truth. You can't possibly imagine how sorry we are."

If they had to talk about this, at least they could do it in private.

Jolene dug her keys from her pocket and headed down the short flight of steps to her apartment. Inside, she left her rapidly cooling breakfast on the table and poured the coffee from the paper cup into her favorite mug. "I don't know what hurts most, the fact that you lied to me for thirty years about who I am, or the fact that you lied about who you are."

Her mother dropped her keys on the table and looked around the apartment. Jolene felt a moment's embarrassment over the as-yet-unpacked boxes stacked in the corners, but she didn't want to care what her mother thought right now. She was through feeling bad because she didn't measure up to some standard that didn't even exist.

"I didn't do it to hurt you," her mother

said, turning back to look at her. "You have to believe that."

"But you *did* hurt me."

"I was trying to protect you."

"From what?"

Margaret's laugh was harsh. "I saw how people treated Billy when we went into the wrong store or restaurant. I didn't want you to have to deal with that."

Jolene was too agitated to sit and her appetite had vanished, so she turned her attention to the closest stack of boxes. "If you felt that way, why did you marry a man who was guaranteed to give you little Indian babies?"

"I loved him."

"But you were ashamed of him." *And of me*.

"If Billy had lived we could have faced it together. He could have taught you all the things you needed to know, but I couldn't do that on my own."

The pain in her mother's eyes forced Jolene to look away.

She pulled a crystal pitcher from the box—a gift from her parents, and one she'd never used. No wonder she hadn't ever felt as if she fit in. Her parents had been trying to make her into something she wasn't since the day she was born.

She thrust the pitcher toward her mother. "Here. Take it back. It doesn't belong here."

"But Dad and I want you to have it."

"Why? I don't cook. I don't entertain. All it does here is collect dust."

Her mother's eyes flashed. "Don't be ridiculous, Jolene. This doesn't change who you are. It doesn't change anything."

"It changes everything," Jolene said, leaving the pitcher on the table. "I'm not who you think I am. I've never been who you want me to be. I never will be."

Her mother clucked her tongue against her teeth impatiently. "Come over here and sit down, Jolene. If this is going to bother you so much, I'll tell you everything you need to know."

How did she do that? How did she manage to make Jolene seem unreasonable? She shook her head and dug into the box again. "I don't want to sit."

Margaret made herself comfortable at the table anyway. "Billy and I met when we were young—both of us. I was just nineteen.

He was twenty and so handsome he took my breath away."

Jolene felt a stab of annoyance in Lawrence's defense. Had her mother ever felt that way about him? Or had he merely been a convenient fallback after Billy Starr's death?

"We met at a dance," Margaret went on softly. "I was there as a guest, he was working. He was dark and mysterious and different from any boy I'd ever met before." She toyed with her wedding ring for a long, silent moment. "We didn't date long, and my family was horribly upset by the marriage. We both had trouble dealing with that. We didn't want them to cause problems for us, but I was too young and too desperately in need of their approval, I guess."

"Then you were unhappy together?"

Margaret tilted her head slightly. "Unhappy? No. Not for a minute. We were head over heels in love. I think the only real fight we ever had was when he insisted on enlisting in the army. He had some big need to make the world a better place."

Jolene's heart gave a painful lurch. "I was like him, and you never told me. Do you know how many nights I lay awake wondering why I couldn't be like Trevor? Why I didn't get all excited about school?"

"Would it have made that much difference?"

"Yes."

"You think so now, but you don't know. I didn't even find out that you were on your way until after he left for Vietnam. He would have been over the moon to find out about you, but—"

"He never even knew about me?"

Margaret shook her head slowly. "I was trying to decide the best way to tell him when I got the news that he was gone."

How could it hurt so much to hear that when she'd never even known he existed until a few days ago? She straightened, clutching a set of plastic bowls to her chest. "Did Billy have any family?"

Margaret nodded and opened her eyes. "He had a mother and two brothers. His father died when he was a teenager. Both of his brothers were married when I knew them, so I'm sure you have cousins by now."

Every piece of information felt like a stone against her chest. "Did they know about me?"

Margaret shook her head. "I should have told them, I know, but I just couldn't. I was so young and frightened, and I was half convinced they'd try to take you away from me. Now, of course, I know better, but you know how it is when you're confused and vulnerable. I wanted to protect you. I couldn't bear to lose you, too."

"Where are they?"

"I—I don't know. Not for sure. I haven't had any contact with them in thirty years."

"So for all you know, they could all be dead, too."

"I'm sure some of them are alive."

"Where were they when you knew them?"

Margaret ran one hand along her arm over and over again. "Here in Tulsa."

"They're here?" That shouldn't have surprised her, but it did. "I could have passed them on the street without even knowing?"

"I suppose it's possible." Margaret raised her eyes slowly. "Are you planning to look for them?"

Finding them would make this all too real. She wasn't ready for that yet. Suddenly overwhelmed, she put the bowls on the counter and broke down the empty box. She could feel her mother watching her, but she didn't look up.

"Can you ever forgive me?"

"I don't know." She carried the box to the front door. "But if I can, it's not going to happen overnight. I need space and time to think. If you love me at all, please give me that."

She left the apartment, door standing wide open, hoping her mother would get the hint and be gone by the time she got back from the Dumpster.

CHAPTER SEVEN

"HEY JO, GIVE ME A HAND with this, would you?"

Ryan's voice brought Jolene out of the fog she'd been lost in since her mother's visit that morning. On the desk in front of her, a screen saver bounced from one side of the computer to the other changing colors every few seconds, and a nearly empty bag of barbecue potato chips lay open but forgotten on the desk.

How long had she been gone this time? Long enough to run over the entire conversation with her mother again and the half-dozen angry voice mail messages from her brother she'd erased.

Abruptly, she became aware of the steady clatter of keyboards and the drone of voices around her as the rest of the special investigations team went about their business.

Jolene had plenty of work to do herself. Three reports waited in her in-box, and the notes she'd made after listening to her voice mail at work littered her desk.

And here she sat, staring off into space. Captain Eisley thought she'd been distracted before. She'd be reassigned to dispatch before the end of the week if she didn't pull herself together.

She'd been trying all afternoon to just get through her shift. As long as she could remember, work had been her refuge. The one place guaranteed to take her mind off everything else. Today, she had trouble remembering she was even here.

Shaking her hand to restore feeling to her numb fingertips, she looked at Ryan and the filthy duffel bag he held in one gloved hand. "What's that?"

"Brady and Mike found it outside that warehouse we've been watching. Captain Eisley wants us to go through it."

"I thought he wanted us to talk to Big Red again."

Ryan looked at her as if she'd lost her mind. "I just told you, nobody can find him. Didn't you hear me?"

He had? "Yeah. Yeah. Sorry. So Eisley wants us to do what with that thing?"

"Look through it. See if it can give us a lead on where Red has gone." Just moving the bag released an odor foul enough to trip her gag reflex, but she was almost grateful. If it was disgusting enough, maybe she'd stop thinking about her personal problems.

She trailed Ryan down the hallway and into one of the examination rooms. He tossed the bag onto a stainless steel table.

"What *is* that?" she demanded, covering her mouth and nose with one hand.

Ryan tossed a box of surgical gloves to her. "Pretty rank, huh? Get your gloves on before you touch anything. Smells like somebody died in there."

Jolene stuffed one hand into a tight-fitting latex glove and eyed the bag warily. "Is that thing big enough to hold a body?"

"That depends on the size of the person." Ryan looked as if he was enjoying her discomfort. He unzipped the bag and pushed the flaps out of the way so they could both see what was inside.

Jolene leaned in to take a look. She could handle as much as the next guy on the team.

She'd been telling everyone that since the day she walked in the door, and she'd go right on saying it until they believed her. She just wished she didn't have to prove it today when exhaustion and emotion were working together to keep her on the edge.

Breathing through his mouth, Ryan poked around in the duffel bag for a minute, sifting through contents that looked as if they'd been doused in some kind of liquid and then rolled in dirt. One after the other, he pulled out two soiled T-shirts, a shoe with a hole in the sole, a pair of pants so dirty she couldn't imagine anyone wearing them and three dog-eared issues of *Playboy*.

Jolene catalogued the items carefully as Ryan looked up from the last item. "Trust Red to have those." His…fondness…for women was well-known around the station, and female officers took extra precautions when they had to talk to him. "Is there anything else in there? What's causing the smell?"

Ryan shook his head and went back to the search. After a few seconds, he barked a laugh and plunged his hand into the bag. He withdrew it a second later holding a dead mouse by the tail. The stench exploded in the air and the control Jolene had been fighting evaporated. Her stomach lurched, and she bolted from the table while the coffee and chips she'd been living on all afternoon rose in her throat.

She could hear Ryan's laughter following her as she raced down the hallway, both hands clamped firmly over her mouth. It would take months to live this down, but she couldn't make herself care.

She ducked into a stall just in time, and emerged a few minutes later, shaky and embarrassed. After rinsing her mouth, she studied her reflection in the mirror. The lack of sleep showed in the dark circles under her eyes, which were dull and almost opaque. Her face seemed strange to her. Whose nose was that? Whose eyes? From which unknown relative had she inherited her chin, her cheeks, her shape, her hair?

She was torn apart by questions and terrified of the answers, but couldn't allow this to paralyze her.

Smoothing the hair away from her face, she squared her shoulders and pushed out into the hall where she found Ryan leaning against the wall and studying the pattern of the carpet at his feet.

He actually looked worried. "You okay Jo-Jo?"

Illogically, his concern irritated her. "I'm fine. Let's get back to work."

He caught her by the arm before she could get more than a couple of steps. "You're not fine. What's going on?"

"Nothing." She tried to pull her arm away, but he held on.

"You've been moody and distracted all day. Whatever it is, why don't you just spill it?"

"I'm not *moody*," she snapped. "I'm fine. Just back off, okay?" She regretted pushing him away the second the words left her mouth. Ryan was the one person she might've been able to confide in, but she could tell by the look on his face that it was too late.

With a brittle shrug, he let go of her arm. "Okay. Have it your way. I just came to tell you that there's somebody here to see you, anyway. Thought you'd want to know."

"Who is it?" she demanded, praying that nobody in her family had decided to ambush her at work.

Ryan shrugged again and started walking toward her.

"Might be the girl from the other night. Seems to think you're the only one who can help her."

"Debra? What is she doing here?"

Ryan pulled a toothpick from his pocket and spent a second or two situating it in his mouth. "No idea. I told her to wait for you out by the elevators." Ryan moved the toothpick from one side of his mouth to the other. "I thought that would be better than letting her wait around Big Red's duffel bag."

Just the thought of that duffel bag made Jolene's stomach lurch again. "Good idea. Thanks. I'll go see what she wants." Grasping eagerly at the distraction, Jolene hurried down the hall.

Two minutes later, she rounded the corner and spotted Debra sitting on a carpeted bench kicking her feet in front of her and humming softly. She wore jeans and a sweater, and her jacket lay on the bench beside her. Her long, dark hair was pulled back in a braid, accentuating the sharp cheekbones and almond-shaped eyes she'd inherited from her father. "Debra? What are you doing here?"

The girl's head popped up and she bounded to her feet. "Is this okay? I mean, coming here like this?"

"I don't know. What's wrong?"

"I don't know where my dad is, and I can't get into the apartment. I didn't know what to do, but then I remembered that card you gave me."

Relieved that the problem wasn't serious, Jolene nodded for her to sit again and sank onto the bench beside her. "Have you tried calling your dad?"

"I don't have a cell phone, and I didn't have any money for a pay phone."

"Well, then, how did you get here?"

"My friend's mom gave me a ride. She took me home from diving practice, and then she brought me here."

Was she telling the truth? She certainly seemed to be, but she'd fooled Jolene once already and Jolene wasn't as good at sensing a lie as she'd once believed.

"Didn't your friend's mom have a cell phone?"

"Not with my dad's number in it."

"Was this the friend who gave the party you went to?"

Debra shook her head quickly. "No, that was somebody else."

"Couldn't you have stayed at their house until your dad got home?"

"I wanted to, but she said they had to go somewhere." The pupils of her eyes began to move rapidly and Jolene suspected that wasn't entirely true.

The question was, what was she going to do about it? Tempting as the idea sounded, stringing the kid up by her toes and leaving her there until she got the idea that lying was bad probably wouldn't fly, either with Mason or the department. "I guess I'm going to have to call your dad and get him to stop by and pick you up, then. Do you know his number at work?"

Debra's gaze shifted away. "He doesn't have one. He works outside all the time."

"Does he have a cell phone?"

"Yeah."

"Do you know that number?"

"No."

"So you're telling me that your dad takes off for work and leaves you home alone, without any way to contact him?"

Debra must have heard the disbelief in

her voice because her gaze settled on a picture on the far wall and her voice grew less confident. "I have it, but it's on speed dial and I lost where he wrote it down."

Yeah. That figured. It seemed to Jolene that the kid was having a great time making up stories. Unfortunately for her, Jolene was in no mood. She leaned forward and put herself in the girl's line of vision. "Listen up, Debra, because I'm only going to say this once. I don't like being lied to. In fact, I really, *really* don't like being lied to. In fact, when I find out that somebody is lying to me, I get really angry. It's hard to like somebody who makes up stuff just to get somebody else in trouble. So think about that and let's go get a Coke out of the machine, and then you tell me again where your dad is, okay?"

The gleam died and Debra's expression went from crafty to subdued in a heartbeat. "Maybe he—"

Jolene stood and held up a hand to stop her. "Not right now. I've had a bad day and I'm not feeling very happy. Let's go get that Coke. I'm sure it will help."

Debra stood reluctantly, grabbed her

jacket and held it in front of her as she shuffled into the elevator beside Jolene. There was something endearing about her, but Jolene couldn't have explained what it was if her life depended on it.

They reached the second floor, and Jolene led the girl into the cafeteria. Several tables were occupied and the acidic smell of old coffee filled the air. Jolene chose a table apart from the others and left Debra there while she fed quarters into the Coke machine. On impulse, she bought a bag of chips and a cookie, then carried everything back to the table and sat where she could look into Debra's eyes.

"Okay, now," she said, passing the food and one can to the girl. "Let's try this again. Where is your dad?"

Debra focused on removing the plastic wrap from the cookie. "He's at work."

"Do you know where he's working?"

"At the county complex out by the university, I think."

Jolene knew that area well. She could probably find him if she wanted to go looking. But since both of her parents would also be there, that was not an area of town she wanted to spend time in. "When does he get home?"

"That depends."

"What time does he *usually* get home?"

Debra shrugged, crumpled the plastic wrap in her fist, and broke the cookie in two. "Maybe seven."

That was just an hour from now, and Jolene's shift would be ending at roughly the same time. She could just drive Debra home—again—but she hated to make a habit of it. She watched two uniformed officers sitting nearby finish their snacks and toss their garbage. "Have you thought about that cell phone number some more?"

Debra's expression grew earnest. "I don't remember it. I have it written down at home, but I can't get in." She dropped her gaze again and added, "I forgot my key."

Finally, the truth. "What about a neighbor? Is there somebody in the complex we can call?"

"I don't know very many people. I don't know their names."

Jolene knew she could call the leasing office. They'd have a spare key, and they could let Debra into her apartment. But something held her back. She ignored the flash of anticipation at the thought of seeing Mason again and told herself she just didn't want to leave Debra alone. "What about that guy who was at your house when I took you home? Your dad's friend. What was his name again?"

"Ike?"

"That's the one."

Debra nibbled one corner of the cookie. "He's not home, and I'm not making that up. He had to go somewhere for a couple of days."

"Is there anybody else? Do you have family nearby? Maybe somebody from the Cherokee Center who could watch you?"

Debra's gaze flew to hers. "My dad would never let me go there."

"Really? Why not?"

"He doesn't like it. He doesn't like any of that stuff."

"What stuff? Cherokee stuff?"

Debra's expression grew solemn. "He gets really mad whenever somebody asks about it."

That was certainly interesting. "Do you know why?"

Debra took another bite of cookie. "My mom said he hates to talk about it. I'm supposed to do a report on my grandparents. Kind of an interview thing, you know? For school?" Her gaze flicked around the room, never quite landing on anything. "I wanted to find out about my dad's family because I don't know anything about them, but my mom said not to count on it. He never talks about them."

Intrigued, Jolene rested her chin in her hand and let herself acknowledge the heritage she shared with this girl. "So you don't know anything about the Cherokee?"

"Not much. I found some books in the library, but they were all just stories about spiders finding fire and rabbits and talking wolves and stuff. It didn't make sense."

"Lots of legends, huh?"

"I guess."

"And your dad won't talk to you about it?"

Debra swept crumbs onto the floor. "I don't know what the big deal is, but he acts like he's...you know...prejudiced or something."

Against himself? His daughter? Could

that even happen? Mason didn't seem like the kind of guy to be that unreasonable, but she barely knew him. "I'm sure that's not it," she told Debra. "Maybe he just doesn't know much about the culture."

Debra took a long drink of Coke and shook her head. "Ike told me that after my grandma died, that old man who raised my dad—Henry?—he taught them all kinds of things. Ike says he was a tribal elder, and he knew all about the history, and he taught my dad. My dad just won't tell *me*."

Another parent who thought he had the right to keep the truth from his daughter just because he didn't like it? And he seemed like such a nice guy. "What about Ike? Can you talk to him?"

Debra nodded slowly. "I can, and I do a little bit, but I'm afraid my dad will get mad."

It was on the tip of Jolene's tongue to tell Debra she shouldn't let that stop her, but some tiny seed of common sense found its way to the surface. No matter what her personal situation, no matter what she thought about Mason's choices, it wasn't her place to incite rebellion in his already mutinous daughter. Not telling the kid about her Cherokee heritage wasn't a crime—even though Jolene thought it ought to be.

"Come with me," she said, standing abruptly.

Debra swept the crumbs from her shirt with the back of her hand. "Where?"

"Upstairs. I need to finish something and let my partner know I'm leaving, then I'll drive you home. But I want you to write down all the phone numbers you need and carry them with you from now on. And *remember your key*."

Debra grabbed her sweater and almost looked worried. "Are you mad at me?"

"No. I'm not mad. This just isn't the best place in the world for a kid, and I'm really busy. I can't stop working to drive you home every time I see you."

The sadness in Debra's sharp little face sent a pang of guilt through Jolene, but it couldn't be helped. The last thing she needed right now was to form an emotional connection to a testy kid and her secretive dad.

CHAPTER EIGHT

TRYING TO HANG ON TO the sanity he had left, Mason flipped through the telephone directory and tried to think of someone else he could call. He'd walked in the door half an hour ago, only to find the house empty and dark. No sign of Debra anywhere. No note. No voice mail message. Nothing. And after the stunt she'd pulled on Friday, he was half-crazy with worry.

He'd already called Brynne Stanton's mother, hoping they'd taken Debra home with them. Brynne's mother wasn't home, but her dad swore that Debra hadn't been with them when they came in after practice. So where *was* she?

His heart thumped ominously in his chest and he stared at the names swimming on the page in front of him. Debra didn't know that many people in Tulsa. She didn't have a list of places she could go. That frightened him a whole lot more than if he'd had a thousand possibilities to choose from.

He flipped pages, found a listing for Coach Walkenhorst and punched the number on the keypad. Just as the phone started to ring, the doorbell rang. He jumped and dropped the phone onto the counter.

Nerves. He swore Debra was going to be the death of him.

Breaking the connection, he strode to the front door, praying that Debra would be there, already planning what he'd say to her if she was. He yanked open the door, saw Debra, and felt such an overwhelming surge of relief, it took a second to recognize Jolene as the woman standing next to her.

When he did, his heart sank. "What happened? Is she in trouble again?"

"She's fine. She asked someone to bring her to the station after practice because she forgot her key."

Mason looked from one to the other. "To the police station? Why didn't you just go to the leasing office? They have a spare key."

"I didn't think of it." Debra stared him in the eye, daring him to pressure her further.

Jolene put a hand on her shoulder and smiled. "Next time she'll remember. But she's promised she won't forget her key again, right, Debra?"

Debra looked away from Mason and her expression changed immediately. "Right."

"You have to admit that coming to the station was better than waiting around outside," Jolene said.

Mason couldn't be sure, but he thought her tone seemed stiff. He must be imagining it—unless he'd offended her last night. He stepped away from the door and motioned for them both to come inside. "If I'd known she was there, I would have come to pick her up. I hope this didn't inconvenience you."

Debra plowed through the door and escaped into her bedroom. Jolene stopped just inside the doorway. "Not really. My shift was almost over when she showed up."

"I'm glad of that, at least. I was just opening a Coke. Can I talk you into joining me?"

The uncertainty on her face did nothing to boost his male ego, but after a moment she nodded. "Sure, why not?"

Wow. She ought to keep his feet firmly planted on the ground. He left her in the living room while he filled two glasses with ice and grabbed two cans from the fridge. By the time he got back she'd made herself comfortable on the couch, pensively studying the box of research Ike still hadn't come by to pick up.

She was so lost in thought, she didn't notice him until he was only a few feet away. She made an effort to smile when he handed her a glass, but the shadows didn't leave her eyes.

"You seem distracted tonight." Considering her lack of enthusiasm for his company, Mason avoided the couch and took his favorite wing chair instead. "Is everything okay?"

She nodded and sat back against the cushions. "I'm fine. Just a little tired. It was a long weekend. I probably shouldn't even be here, but I wanted to talk with you about Debra."

He didn't like the sound of that. "What about her?"

"She talked to me at the station this afternoon. This is none of my business, so if I'm overstepping, please say so. But are you aware that she's interested in learning about her Cherokee heritage?"

Everything inside him grew cold. "You're right. It's none of your business."

"She thinks you're prejudiced—against her. Do you realize that?"

"Against her?" Mason barked a laugh and cracked open his Coke. "How I feel about my past has nothing to do with Debra."

"Well, that's how she sees it. I wouldn't say anything, but you seem worried about her and I thought you should know. I think she may be acting out because she thinks you're ashamed of her."

He waved away her concern. "That's ridiculous. She knows better."

"I'm not sure she does." Jolene leaned to put her glass on the coffee table. "She *told* me she thinks you're prejudiced. That was her word, not mine."

Mason tried to laugh, but the sound died in his throat. "Against myself?"

"Believe it or not, it's not that uncommon. I run into it in my line of work quite often. I've dealt with people who hate some aspect of the life they've led or they're angry over the way people react to them, but they look around them and see other people from the same background doing or saying things that make the reaction they hate seem almost justified. They start thinking if it weren't for that guy, I wouldn't be treated this way, I guess."

"And you think that's what I'm doing."

"I don't know, and if it weren't for Debra I wouldn't care."

She must have realized how cold that sounded because her face flushed and she backpedaled. "I didn't mean that the way it sounded. I just meant that I'm really not the type of person to come barging into your house, telling you how I think you should feel. I'm really only mildly obnoxious."

He actually caught himself smiling at that—surprising, considering how uptight the subject usually made him. "For what it's worth, I'm not ashamed of my daughter, but I have good reasons for avoiding my past."

"I'm sure you do." She took a deep breath and reached for her glass again, but she stared at it for a long time as if she was trying to come to some decision. "I see that the box is still here," she said at last. "I wonder if you'd let me look at that article I saw the other day."

"Which article is that?"

"The one about the people who founded

the Cherokee Communal Center. There was a picture of your—of the guy who raised you. And a couple—?"

Mason nodded. "I remember, I just don't understand."

Jolene smiled wryly. "Don't feel bad, you're not alone. Would you mind?"

More than she could possibly imagine, but he didn't think refusing would make him sound reasonable and intelligent. He dug through the paperwork for the clipping she wanted and glanced at it as he passed it to her, curious.

The slight trembling of her hand as she took the clipping from him made him even more curious. She studied the images intently for a long time, before she looked up, startled, as if she'd just remembered that she wasn't alone. "Would it be possible to get a copy of this?"

"Anything's possible. Do you mind if I ask why you want it?"

Very slowly, Jolene put the clipping on the table in front of her. "I'd rather not say."

Mason watched her expression carefully. "Is it about a case?"

Her eyes registered surprise. "No. Nothing like that."

"You know one of the people in the photograph?"

"I—" She broke off and shook her head. "No." The flush on her cheeks made Mason suspect she wasn't being entirely honest. "I thought maybe I knew one of the people in the picture, but I was mistaken."

Billy Starr was probably dead before she was born, and Mason figured he knew everybody Henry did, so that narrowed it down somewhat. "You know where to find Billy Starr's wife?" Ike would love that. Maybe it would even get Mason off the hook.

Jolene looked as if she might deny it, then said. "I might."

"Why didn't you say something the other night?"

"I didn't realize who she was at the time."

"But you're sure now?"

"I think so."

"Do you know her well? Do you think she'd talk to Ike? He'd think the gods were smiling on him for sure if he could get an interview with her."

Jolene's hesitation turned to something a lot stronger. "I don't think she'd want to be interviewed. She's…moved on with her life, and I don't think she'd welcome the intrusion."

"You could ask, couldn't you?"

Jolene shook her head again and stood. "Forget I said anything, okay? It's really not something I can talk about."

Mason was intrigued by her discomfort and dying to know what had caused it, but she'd allowed him his privacy so he couldn't very well badger her. "I'm sorry I pressured you. Sit down. Finish your Coke, at least."

"No. Thanks. I shouldn't have bothered you in the first place. It was a mistake."

She was across the room and out the door before he could stop her. For the second time in less than a week, Mason watched her rush down the stairs. A minute later, he saw her 4Runner heading toward the opposite side of the complex.

Interesting. Something had spooked her, that was for sure. But what?

And what possible interest could she have in the Center and its founders?

THREE MINUTES LATER, Jolene pulled into her covered parking space and pounded the steering wheel with the heels of her hands.

Once wasn't enough, so she did it again. And again—this time hard enough to make her wince.

What was *wrong* with her? The look on Mason's face when she left had said it all. He thought she was crazy. Even worse, he felt *sorry* for her. There was nothing Jolene hated as much as pity. Except, maybe, being lied to. And feeling out of control.

Overwhelmed she hit the steering wheel once more, and sank against the seat. Her eyes burned with the tears she'd been fighting for the past two days, but she refused to give in to them. Anger she could handle. She knew what to do with it, how to channel it, how to come out on the other side of it in one piece. This incredible, painful sadness that filled her twenty-four hours a day was new to her, and she had no idea how to live with it.

From inside her pocket, her cell phone rang. She dug it out and snarled, "Preston."

"It's about time," Trevor said. "I've been waiting for you to come home forever. Where are you?"

Instantly wary, Jolene sat up and checked the cars parked nearby. Sure enough, one row over she spotted Trevor's truck. The cab looked empty, so she took a chance that he hadn't seen her, jerked the 4Runner into gear and pointed it toward the street. "Running errands. Where are you?"

"Sitting on your front porch. I've been trying to call you since Saturday. Why haven't you called me back?"

"Because I know why you're calling, and I don't want to talk about it."

"Mom's been crying since you left. Non-stop."

"I saw her this morning," Jolene said, pulling out of the parking lot and into traffic.

"Yeah, she said you practically kicked her out."

"We'd said everything there was to say. Don't feel too sorry for her. She's hardly the victim here."

"Yeah. I know. Look, Jo, I'm sorry. I really don't know what to say. But it doesn't make any difference. You know that, don't you?"

"Maybe not to you, but it makes a pretty big difference to me."

"Okay. Granted. But it doesn't make any difference in how I feel about you, or how

Mom does. Or Dad, either. I mean, it's always been this way, it's just that you didn't know—right?"

Jolene's heart turned over in her chest. "Did *you* know?"

"No, but they did. That's all I meant. Dad's always known that you weren't—you know what I mean."

"That I'm not his?"

There was an uncomfortable silence. "Yeah," Trevor said at last. "I guess so. But come on, Jo, you know how Dad feels about you."

"Said the guy who didn't just find out that Dad's not even related to him." Something large and hard lodged in her throat.

"But nothing's changed."

It was the same thing her mother had said, but how could they be so blind? "*Everything's* changed," Jolene argued. "Can't you understand that? I'm not even your sister, I'm your half sister. I'm not related to Aunt Betty or Grandma and Grandpa or the cousins. I've got the blood of some stranger running through my veins, and the people I'm related to I've never even seen before." Her frustration grew to match the lump in her throat. "Even my medical history isn't really mine. How do you think that makes me feel?"

"I know it's hard—"

"It's not 'hard,'" Jolene snapped. "It's impossible." She turned a corner too fast and slammed on her brakes to avoid rear-ending a slow-moving Saturn. "I can't deal with this, Trevor, especially not while I'm driving. I don't know what to think and I don't know what to feel except that sometimes I'm so angry I can't even stand to be inside my own skin. When I let myself really think about it, I want to hurt something. I've never felt like this before, and it scares me."

"I know, but if you'd just come out to the house and talk to them…"

She pulled to the side of the road and leaned her head back against the seat. "I can't go back to that house, and I'm not ready to talk to them again. I have nothing to say." Sadness overwhelmed her when she realized how true that was. There really was nothing she wanted to say to the parents who had raised her and who, until just a few days ago, she would have done anything for.

"You're going to have to talk to them

sometime," Trevor said gently. "You might as well do it now. Let's work this out as a family, the way we always do."

Jolene pressed her forehead against the cool steering wheel. It felt so good, she turned her head and leaned her cheek on it. "I know you think I'm wrong, but I can't change what I feel. They lied to me about the biggest thing there is, and they would have kept lying if I hadn't stumbled across the truth."

"Jolene—"

But she was finished. There was nothing more to say, and she was through repeating herself. They weren't listening anyway.

Jolene wedged her cell phone into the cup holder between the seats. Aware of a pulsing pain in her hands and another in her head, she shifted into drive and pulled away from the curb.

The tires squealed in protest, but she ignored them. She knew what she was doing. Driving had always been a release for her, and it wasn't as if she was driving recklessly. There was hardly any traffic along this street, anyway.

She jammed her foot down on the accelerator and tightened her grip on the wheel, waiting for the rush of adrenaline that usually came when she drove a little too fast or pushed the envelope in some other way.

Her cell phone rang again, but she ignored it and the call eventually transferred to voice mail. That would mean another message. More guilt, more anger, more confusion.

Jolene would give anything if she could just turn back the clock. If she could wake up tomorrow morning and discover that the past few days had been a nightmare. She'd always been a realist, and she'd always been proud of that, but she would have changed happily if it meant she could get her life back.

Up ahead, a traffic light changed. Jolene judged the distance, decided she was too close to stop, and pressed the accelerator harder. The car shot forward just as the light turned red, but she sailed through the intersection before the drivers on the cross street could get their feet on the gas.

She pulled her foot from the accelerator and the car began to slow, but not before a cop in a black-and-white unit half a block behind flipped on his overhead lights and siren, and pulled into the sparse traffic behind her.

CHAPTER NINE

NEARLY AN HOUR LATER, Jolene crossed the smoke-filled interior of McGillicuddy's Lounge and tossed the ticket "Officer Friendly" had given her onto the bar. There were bars closer to the station, but Ryan preferred McGillicuddy's. It was close to home and far enough from work to let him make the emotional shift from hard-ass narcotics officer to loving husband and daddy.

She hadn't consciously planned on coming here, but after driving away with the ticket, she'd made a detour on the chance that Ryan would still be here.

She hitched herself onto a faded Naugahyde stool while Ryan gave the ticket a quick once-over and turned a quizzical glance on her. "What's this?"

"Speeding ticket." Ron, the burly biker-type who owned the bar, came to see what she wanted. Now that her spirits were even further down the toilet, she ordered a margarita instead of something more sensible like beer.

"You were going twenty over," Ryan pointed out, as if maybe she didn't know that already. "And you ran a red light?"

"The light turned yellow. I judged the distance and thought I was too close to stop. Officer Friendly saw things a little differently."

Laughing through his nose, Ryan tossed the ticket back to her. "Captain Eisley's going to pass a kidney stone when he finds out. You know that, don't you?"

Her drink arrived, so she pushed a ten across the bar toward Ron, got rid of the straw and filled her mouth with tequila, crushed ice and salt. "Gee, thanks, Ryan," she said when she could speak again. "I forgot all about his rule that we keep our noses clean. But you can't blame me really. He only says it a hundred times a day."

She took another drink and wondered what Ryan would do if she just hauled off and hit him. On second thought, forget that. Ryan would hit back.

He drained the last of his beer, signaled for another, and leaned on the bar. "Ready to talk to me?"

A margarita on an empty stomach was a bad idea, so she leaned across the bar to grab a bag of chips, held it up to show Ron and dropped a dollar on the counter.

"Jo? What is it?"

She tore open the bag. "I don't know what you're talking about."

"There's something eating at you. What is it?"

She shrugged. "Nothing. I just wish we'd been able to nail Zika the other night. All that work down the drain because of some kids. I hate that."

Ryan nodded slowly, but he didn't look convinced. "Yeah. We all do. But we'll get him. His luck can't hold forever."

Jolene laughed bitterly. "Why? Because we're the good guys?"

"Something like that."

"You're a dreamer, Ryan. We don't get to win just because we wear the white hats. Life doesn't work that way."

"You used to think it did."

She made a face. "I was never *that* naive."

"I didn't say you were naive," Ryan said. "I just meant that you had faith in the system. The good guys win, the bad guys go to jail. It's why we're here, doing what we do."

Jolene laughed and studied the lime in her glass. "We're here doing what we do because somebody has to."

"And that's us." Ryan pushed his beer out of the way and hitched his stool closer. "You've been acting weird for a couple of days. Now you're speeding and running red lights…What's going on?"

Maybe she *should* tell him. He was her partner. Her friend. It would be nice to have someone to talk to about this. Sure, admitting that she had doubts and insecurities might make her look weak in Ryan's eyes, but so would going off her game for no apparent reason. And wouldn't anybody in her shoes be thrown by the things she'd been told this week? Even Captain Eisley might do a double take if somebody told him to stop celebrating Oktoberfest and do a war dance instead.

She pulled in a deep breath and let it out slowly. "Okay, you're right. There is something—" Before she could finish, a shout erupted somewhere behind her followed by the unmistakable sounds of a scuffle.

Ryan was on his feet in half a second, their conversation forgotten. He was a good cop. A week ago, Jolene would have been on her feet right beside him. Today, she had to drag her attention away from the turmoil inside her just to register the trouble.

Captain Eisley would have a field day with this if he found out—and why shouldn't he? No matter how Jolene felt about it personally, she knew one thing as well as she knew her own name—there's no place on the force for a self-absorbed cop.

The trouble was over almost as soon as it began. Two men, one tall and blond, the other stockier, dark-haired and vaguely familiar to Jolene, settled back at their table, giving each other looks and posturing a bit to make sure the other knew he hadn't won the battle.

Clearly unhappy, Ryan settled back on his stool and linked his hands together on the bar. "Some backup, Jo-Jo. Where the hell were you?"

"Sorry. Anything serious?"

He lifted one shoulder. "Some drunk Indian wanting to pound in the head of his white friend. Nothing to worry about."

Jolene caught her breath. She'd heard Ryan talk like that before. She'd heard others on the force toss it off without thinking at least a thousand times. Before tonight, it hadn't meant anything to her.

Mason's image flashed through her head, followed closely by Debra's. She thought of the smiling faces of Billy Starr and Henry Owle in the photograph she'd seen, and of her own face staring back at her from the mirror.

She hated thinking that she'd nursed any prejudices at all, but she'd been as guilty as the next guy of not calling it when she saw it in others. And she'd had the nerve to come across all high-and-mighty with Mason.

"So you were saying?"

Much as she liked Ryan and respected him, hearing him talk disparagingly about a drunk Indian tonight killed something inside her. The desire to explain what she was going through withered right along with it. There was no way she could tell him his partner was Indian, especially since she still didn't know how she felt about it, or how it might change her.

She watched the familiar-looking man leave his table and stumble a little on his way to the men's room, cell phone glued to his ear as he walked. Probably just someone she'd busted on a minor drug charge, she decided, and looked back to find Ryan eyeing her chips.

Nudging the bag toward him, she shook her head. "I don't know. I think maybe it's just stress. Losing that Zika bust bothered me more than it should."

One of Ryan's eyebrows arched. "That's it?"

"That's it."

"Bullshit. There's something else. You were just about to tell me what it was. Don't stop now."

"It's nothing."

"One failed bust had you sitting here on your butt while I went over there into God knows what?" Ryan demanded with a jerk of his head toward the back of the bar.

"I said I was sorry."

"Fat lot of good sorry's gonna do me if we're out there on the job someday and you can't be bothered to back me up."

"I'll back you," Jolene insisted. "It won't happen again."

Ryan snorted a laugh and shook his head in disbelief. "Oh. Oh, good. See, for a minute there, I was worried. But I feel all better now. Kind of warm and fuzzy inside."

Jolene shoved her drink away and stood. "Don't be an ass, Fielding."

"Then don't bullshit me."

"I'm not!" Jolene shouted. She was furious with Ryan for being such a jerk, even more furious with herself for lying. Why couldn't she just tell him? What did it matter what he thought of her? What did it say about her that she cared?

She took in the doubt and suspicion on Ryan's broad, open face and decided to get the hell out of there before she did something she'd regret. "Why don't you have another beer?" she suggested bitterly, snatching her keys from the bar and swallowing enough margarita to give her brain freeze. "You're not nearly drunk enough."

She heard Ryan shout something as she marched across the bar and pushed outside, but she didn't stop. He was right about one thing. She wasn't herself, and she didn't trust this person she'd turned into.

She stood in the cool night air for a minute

trying to pull herself together, then unlocked the 4Runner and climbed in behind the wheel. But she couldn't make herself turn the key. She hadn't had enough to drink to register on a Breathalyzer, but she'd nearly run over Mason last night, nearly rear-ended that Saturn earlier and she'd racked up two moving violations on the way here. She'd be stupid to risk more.

So her life had come to this. She dragged out her cell phone and called for a cab, then sat back to wait with her eyes closed. In the past two days, her well-ordered life had turned into something she barely recognized. She'd turned into someone she didn't know. She'd lost her family, and she was damn close to losing her friend.

Somehow she had to regain control, before she spontaneously combusted and destroyed everything around her.

CHAPTER TEN

HUNCHED DEEP into her department-issue slicker, Jolene trudged across the parking lot of the old GemCrest Toys warehouse two steps behind Ryan. A light rain had been falling since morning, and they'd been out in the elements since their shift began, searching for a slimy drug dealer and some-times-informant known as OC.

They still hadn't found a trace of Big Red and, while users and pushers could crawl into holes and disappear in the blink of an eye, Jolene was starting to worry about this one. Raoul Zika was a dangerous man. He could be a deadly enemy.

Word on the street was that OC had been seen arguing with Big Red before he disap-peared. Maybe it was true, maybe it wasn't. Some people would say anything if they thought it would benefit them.

Even if OC knew where to find Big Red, Jolene had serious doubts about whether he'd talk to them. The guy blew hot and cold, depending on the day, how long ago he'd had his last fix and how desperately he wanted cash to buy his next one.

A day like this one was miserable enough when everything was going well, but Ryan had barely spoken to her since their argument at McGillicuddy's three nights earlier, and the atmosphere inside their department-issue Crown Victoria had been cold as a winter night.

She and Ryan had spent their fair share of time in miserable conditions before, but today it seemed as if Ryan was choosing all the worst places to look. If she didn't know better, she'd think he was punishing her.

Jolene dodged a puddle and realized that her feet were numb. To make matters worse, her pants were wet almost to the knee and her fingers had gone stiff from the cold. But she'd die before she complained. "You really think we're going to find OC here?" she said to Ryan's back.

He glanced over his shoulder at her, his eyes cold. "If he's not here, we'll keep looking—unless it's too hard on you. Do you have a problem with it?"

Maybe she *wasn't* imagining things. He really could be a jerk sometimes. "*I'm* not the one with the problem," she growled.

Ryan abruptly stopped walking. "What the hell is that supposed to mean?"

To avoid plowing into him, Jolene stepped to one side, and this time she landed in a puddle of ankle-deep water. Swearing under her breath, she found dry land again and pulled off her shoe so she could dump the water. "It means that you've been acting like an ass ever since the other night," she snarled. "You can let up anytime now."

Ryan started walking again. "I don't know what you're talking about."

Seriously annoyed, Jolene hopped on one foot to keep up as she got her shoe back on. "You're upset because I won't get all weepy and confess that something's bothering me."

"I'm upset because you refuse to be honest with me."

He had a point, but Jolene didn't want him to be right. "Why is it so important to you, Fielding? You have some twisted need to be the big strong man or something?"

"Stuff it, Preston," Ryan shot back over his shoulder. "Just keep your mind on the job."

"My mind *is* on the job," she insisted. "You're the one who's acting all pissy."

Ryan spun around. "Drop it before you say something we both regret." His eyes were narrow and his jaw set. She'd seen that expression before, but always when they were dealing with pushers or some strung-out mother who'd abandoned a child in her search for a fix. He resumed walking.

Jolene knew she'd crossed a line. She'd worked for eighteen long months to earn his trust, and she'd blown it in just a couple of days. And for what? The anger churning around inside her had nothing to do with Ryan.

Standing in the middle of the parking lot, waterlogged from head to toe, she sighed in resignation. "I didn't mean to insult you the other night. You're right, something is bothering me. But it's…it's personal and tough to talk about."

Disgusted, Ryan didn't even break stride, his rigid shoulders a barrier between them.

"If I could tell you about it, I would."

He whipped back again so quickly, she flinched. "There's no such thing as personal when you're a police officer, Jo. Not between partners. What affects you, affects me. Don't you get that?"

She nodded miserably. "Yes, but—"

"If you're distracted in the wrong situation, I'm dead. It's as simple as that. If you don't understand that, we've got a problem I'm not sure we can fix."

He couldn't have said anything more hurtful. "You're right," she said again. "I'm sorry."

Something flickered in his eyes, but it was gone before she could identify it. "That's it?"

"What do you want me to do, grovel?"

He almost smiled at that. "That would be a good start."

That near-smile got her blood pumping again. "Yeah, well, you have to know *that's* not gonna happen. All I can tell you is that I know I need to deal with this issue so it's not a danger to either of us."

"And?"

How would he react to learning that she was half Cherokee? Would it matter? Would he try to pretend that it didn't?

"I'll tell you," she conceded with effort, "but not here." She glanced at the warehouse's broken windows and the door sagging on its hinges and shivered. "I'm freezing my butt off. How about I confess everything over something hot to drink?"

Ryan dipped his head once. "Let's check this place out and then call in a forty-five."

She needed a coffee break as much as she needed to release some of the tension she'd been carrying around. Really, she ought to be grateful that Ryan was willing to listen. She couldn't keep holding it all inside, and who else could she confide in? As they had countless times over the past few days, her thoughts strayed to Mason. But that was ridiculous. She barely knew him, and it would be a giant stretch of her imagination to call him a friend.

Ryan was right about one thing. She *had* been distracted lately, and being distracted in a place like this could be deadly. She stepped into the warehouse and shook the water from her hair and jacket.

These were the moments her parents hated most about her job.

She wondered what Billy Starr would

think of her and the life she'd chosen, then immediately tried to wipe that question out of her mind. She didn't want to care about that, and she couldn't let her personal life interfere with her job again.

With her eyes adjusted to the dim light inside, she ran a quick glance around the seemingly vacant warehouse. To the uninitiated, the cavernous room appeared deserted, but this building housed an active and thriving drug community that Jolene and Ryan felt certain was part of Zika's operation.

Thick layers of dust covered almost every surface, rusted chains coiled in one corner and mounds of old cardboard boxes disintegrated slowly in the building's moist interior. Only a little light spilled through the broken windows on the first-floor level, and the walking was treacherous.

This wasn't Jolene's first time inside, or Ryan's, either, but neither allowed familiarity to make them reckless. They moved together cautiously, Jolene keeping an eye on the right side while Ryan watched the left, each aware of every sound and every movement.

As they climbed the stairs to the second floor, odors she didn't want to identify floated up from the stairwell, and she could make out new colorful graffiti on the walls. At the top of the stairs, she saw a young girl, no more than seventeen, slink into the shadows, and she thought of Debra. Some of these kids ended up here because nobody cared, but others left grieving, frightened families behind—parents and siblings who would give anything to have their sister or brother, their son or daughter come home clean and drug-free.

Jolene hated to think of someone as young and innocent as Debra getting caught up in a world like this one. She'd seen mothers abandon children in search of drugs, children prostituting themselves for the junk they craved, and more ugliness done by one human being to another than anyone should see in a lifetime. Mason was right to be worried. If she ever saw him again, she should probably tell him so.

Faint music played somewhere in the distance, whispered conversations hushed as she and Ryan moved across the second floor. She heard someone crying softly, someone else swearing. The smell of vomit was strong.

They found OC in the far corner, his eyes red-rimmed and vacant in his gaunt face, his pale hair slick with grease and dirt. He rolled his eyes and curled onto his side as if that might convince them to leave.

"Hey there, OC," Ryan said, nudging him with the toe of his boot. "How's it hanging?"

"Go away."

Jolene hunkered down and at eye level with him. "Sorry. Can't do that. Looks like you're using again, OC. What's up with that?"

OC shook his head. Stains dulled his teeth and dark circles rimmed his eyes. "Somebody must be lying to you. I'm clean."

"Yeah," Ryan said, "you look clean."

"It's true. I haven't used in a long time."

Ryan shared a look of disbelief with Jolene and gave OC another nudge. "You sure about that, buddy?"

"Sure I'm sure." OC flopped onto his back and tried to focus on their faces. "I'm being straight with you, man. I don't do that shit anymore."

"Well, that's good. I'm proud of you." Ryan bent, grabbed OC's arm and tugged him to his feet. "We're both proud, aren't we, Jolene?"

Jolene took his other arm and tried not to notice how bad he smelled. "Sure we are. Real proud. But the only trouble is, you don't look like you're being straight with us. How long has it been since you shot up?"

OC managed to look outraged for a split second before his knees buckled. He struggled to keep his balance—not an easy task, even with a person on either arm to hold him up. "I don't know. What time is it now?"

Ryan's laugh bounced off the walls. A head popped up from behind a nearby crate, and Jolene heard the telltale *swish* of someone scuffling deeper into hiding behind her. "That's what I figured," Ryan said. "You're lucky we're not really looking for you."

That got OC's attention. "Who do you want?"

"Big Red," Jolene said. "You seen him lately?"

OC shook his head and tried to get back to the floor. "Nope."

Jolene held his arm tightly, forcing him to stay on his feet—sort of. "Are you sure? I thought you were a friend of his."

"I know who he is," OC admitted, "but I wouldn't say we're friends."

"That's not what we've heard," Ryan said. "We heard that the two of you are tight. So think again and see if you remember seeing him around in the past week or so."

"What do you want him for?"

"We just need to ask him a couple of questions. When did you see him last?"

OC wiped his nose with the back of his hand. "I dunno. Weeks ago."

"We heard you were talking to him on Saturday," Jolene told him.

The man's beady eyes narrowed. "Where'd you hear that?"

"Around." She nodded for Ryan to let go and planted herself in front of OC. "Matter of fact," she said, switching tactics abruptly, "we heard you were the last person to see Big Red." She flicked something from his shoulder and straightened his collar—feminine gestures that some men responded to without realizing it. "A couple of patrol officers found his bag just outside the warehouse, here. Looks like all his stuff is still in it, and it's not like Red to leave that bag behind. That makes us worry."

OC's eyes shifted from one to the other. "You think something's happened to him?"

"That's what we're asking you."

"I don't know. Why would I know?"

"Aw, come on, OC, don't sell yourself short." Ryan leaned against a clean patch of wall and crossed one foot over the other. "I'll bet you have plenty to say. Are you on Zika's payroll now?"

OC's lip curled to reveal his stained teeth. "No."

"Are you sure? Maybe Zika asked you to do him a favor and get Big Red out of the way. Maybe that's why you were talking to Red right before he disappeared."

"That's *not* what happened."

"Then what *did* happen?" Jolene asked.

"I don't *know*. Nothing. You're just making stuff up, trying to get me to cop to something I didn't do so you can bust my chops, aren't you?"

"Not today," Ryan said with a cool grin.

"Then leave me alone. I don't have anything to say."

"Now, see, that's where we disagree. I think you should tell us what you were doing at the middle school yesterday afternoon."

Panic darted across OC's ugly face. "I wasn't at the school. Who told you I was?"

"A little bird," Jolene said. "You just can't imagine how disappointed we were, either. Especially after that nice, long talk we had about what we were going to do with you if we found you by the school again. I thought we had an understanding."

"We did. We *do*," OC insisted. "I *wasn't* at any school."

Ryan leaned in close and spoke just above a whisper. "Tell us what you know about Raoul Zika and Big Red. Maybe we'll believe you."

"That's blackmail."

Ryan shrugged. "We prefer to call it creative bargaining. What do you say, OC? What do you have for us?"

Beads of sweat popped out on OC's nose and forehead. "I've got nothin'," he said. "I don't know nothin'. Nobody does."

"Nobody?"

OC looked her in the eye. "Nobody. Zika's operation is tight. He don't let just anybody in, and he don't let nobody out easy, either. But anything could have happened to Red. He's a damn junkie."

"Isn't that the pot calling the kettle black?" Ryan's mouth thinned. "Come on, OC. We know you're dealing for Zika. We know Red's been on the string, too. Now Red's missing, and word is that Zika had you take care of him. If that's not what happened, then tell us so we can put Zika away."

OC lifted his chin defiantly. "I don't even know Raoul Zika."

"Sure you do," Ryan said, "Think again. See if you can remember."

What little light there'd been in OC's eyes dimmed. "I know who he is. Everybody does. But I don't know *him,* I don't deal for him and I didn't take care of Big Red."

"I'll bet you know something about his operation, though, don't you?" Jolene pressed. "Why don't you just tell us what you know?"

OC backed a step or two away, his voice dropped to barely above a whisper. "I don't know nothin'. I don't even like saying the man's name aloud."

"Why are you afraid of him?" Jolene

asked. "Because you know what happened to Red?"

OC's expression grew blank. "I don't know. I don't have nothin' to say to you. Nothin'. You got that?" He backed farther away, stumbling over his own two feet. "The two of you coming around here and talking like that is going to get *me* dead."

He was so obviously panicked, Ryan held up both hands in a sign of surrender. With the pressure off, OC lurched into the shadows and disappeared.

"He knows something," Ryan muttered under his breath.

Jolene nodded, but she didn't speak until they were outside again. No telling who might be listening, and they'd already put OC in enough danger. "OC's always afraid of his own shadow," she said as they plunged through the rain toward the car, "but I'd say Zika's been making his presence felt."

"That's how I read it," Ryan agreed. "I don't like the feel of this. I don't think we're going to see Big Red alive."

Jolene would have given anything to argue with him, but she was afraid he was right.

They reached the Crown Vic, and Ryan stopped with one hand on the driver's door. "Ready for that coffee?"

For the first time in days, her family situation almost felt like a respite. She forced a smile and nodded. "Sure. Unless you'd rather head back to the station and see what the captain says."

"Nice try, Preston, but you're not getting out of this one. There's nothing we can do for Red except keep looking, and nothing we can do for OC if he won't ask for help. Now, get in the car. I'm all ready for a story."

CHAPTER ELEVEN

HALF AN HOUR LATER, Jolene gratefully clutched her cup of coffee in both hands and let the warmth seep into her bones. They'd settled into their usual booth at The Blue Plate, a popular diner not far from the GemCrest warehouse. They sat near the front of the diner, in a booth that gave them a clear view out the window—just in case.

Ryan poured ketchup onto his plate and sopped a couple of fries in it. "You sure you don't want half?" he asked, nodding toward the chicken avocado sandwich he'd ordered.

Jolene shook her head and dipped the tines of her fork into her salad dressing. She could already feel the waistband of her favorite pants cinched too tight around her waist. She couldn't afford to keep giving in to temptation. Why couldn't she have been one of those women whose dainty appetite disappeared under stress?

"I'm fine," she said when she realized Ryan was still waiting for an answer. "This salad is all I want."

"Now I *know* something's wrong." He stuffed another couple of fries into his mouth and spoke around them. "So what is it?"

Jolene vowed she wasn't going to let this make her emotional. Doing her best to look as if it was no big deal, she said, "I found out the other day that my mother was married before she met my dad."

Ryan's eyes flashed to her face. "You didn't know?"

"I didn't know."

"Wow. So how'd you find out?"

"One of those weird coincidences." Someone fed quarters into the jukebox and an Alan Jackson song filled the air. "I happened across a photo of my mom standing next to this guy outside some building about thirty years ago. It was in a newspaper article, and the caption said this Margaret person was married to this guy. It never occurred to me that it might actually *be* her. I just thought it was a weird coincidence that someone else named Margaret could look so much like my mother."

"You're sure it wasn't?"

Jolene took a bite of salad and made a face. What she *really* wanted was a chocolate-banana shake. And onion rings. Large. "No, it wasn't. I mentioned it to her last time I was over there, one thing led to another, and she told me the truth."

Ryan stopped chewing. "So she was married before and she never told you. That's why you're all wigged out?"

Did she have to tell him the rest? Or would this much be enough? Jolene stared at the lettuce speared onto her fork, then slowly set it aside. "I also found out that my mom had a kid with her first husband."

Ryan blinked. "No kidding! Boy or girl?"

"Girl."

"So you have a long-lost sister out there somewhere?"

"Not exactly."

"The baby died or something?"

"No, she lived. According to my mother, that baby is me."

Ryan swallowed wrong, coughed a couple of times and had to chug half a glass of water before he could speak again. "You?" he got out at last. "You're kidding, right?"

Jolene wasn't sure whether his reaction made her feel better or worse. "No," she said, "but I wish I was."

"And she never told you?"

"She didn't seem to think that was necessary."

He sat back in his seat, wagged his head in disbelief and let out a low whistle. "That's heavy. No wonder you've been acting so strange lately."

Jolene actually managed a weak smile. "Thanks."

"So what does your mother have to say about all of this?"

"Not much. She was angry with me for asking questions, and then she got all weepy."

"What has she told you about your biological father?"

"He died in Vietnam before I was born."

"What about his family?"

Jolene felt herself shutting down inside, as she did every time she thought about Billy Starr's people. "What about them?"

"Who are they?"

"I have no idea."

"You haven't asked?" Ryan stared at her as if she'd just sprouted wings but refused to fly. "You could have uncles and aunts and cousins and God only knows what else out there you don't know anything about."

And he thought that was a good thing? Jolene caught herself eyeing his fries and considered ordering some for herself. "I might, but it's weird to be related to people I don't even know. It's not something I want to think about yet."

Ryan must have noticed the direction of her gaze because he scooped a mound of fries onto her plate. "You're going to have to, Jo."

It had been days since he'd used her nickname. "I'll find them—eventually."

"Eventually? What are you talking about? I know you. Unanswered questions bug the hell out of you. You aren't going to be happy until you know exactly what your situation is and, in the meantime, you'll drive both of us crazy and probably piss the captain off in your spare time."

Jolene debated telling Ryan about Eisley's threat, but decided to keep that particular humiliation private for the time being. Under normal circumstances what Ryan said about her curious nature was true, but this time the unanswered questions had the power to change her life, and that made everything different. "I won't bring it to work with me," she promised. "It won't affect you at all."

One eyebrow arched with skepticism. "The way it hasn't the past few days?"

"Cut me some slack, Ryan. I just found out about this. I'll get it under control, I promise."

"You can't promise that. Not until you know exactly what you're dealing with. Talk to your mother."

"Easy for you to say. It's not your life falling apart or your mother who spent the past thirty years lying."

His understanding changed to exasperation in the blink of an eye. "Explain how you're going to get this 'thing' under control. Are you expecting to just wake up one morning and magically feel better?"

"Of course not. Don't be ridiculous. I'll figure something out, though."

"What about your dad? Can you talk to him?"

"He knew about this all along. He lied, too."

Ryan frowned in thought. "Maybe you should talk to Richard Wong."

"The department shrink? Are you serious?" That would only make the rest of the unit think she was unstable, and give Captain Eisley fodder he didn't need. "No thanks."

"You have a better suggestion?"

One idea did occur to her, but it was so preposterous, she ignored it. Mason Blackfox was *not* the solution to this problem. "I just need time," she said again. "That's all. Let me come to terms with this in my own way."

"Not while I'm your partner." Ryan rested his arms on the table and stared at her. "Sorry, but with Zika stirred up again and Big Red missing, that's a luxury neither of us can afford."

"Nobody wants to put Zika away more than I do. Trust me."

"I wish I could," Ryan said, his voice low, "but I need more than that."

The hair on the back of Jolene's neck stood up. "What's that supposed to mean?"

"It means either you get your head straight and do it fast, or I'm going to talk to Eisley about assigning me a new partner."

Jolene felt the blood drain from her face. If Ryan went to Eisley, that would just about guarantee that she'd be transferred out of the squad. "You're giving me an ultimatum?"

"I'm looking out for myself. You're a good partner, Jolene, but I'm not putting myself at risk if I don't have to. I've got a wife and kids to think about. You shouldn't be out there while you're dealing with this."

The anger she'd been trying to keep under control since that day in her mother's study erupted. How dare he threaten her? How *dare* he try to take away the only thing she had left? "I'm sorry my personal crisis is inconvenient for you. Next time somebody wants to detonate a bomb in the middle of my life, I'll have them check with you first."

"Yeah, that's it, Jo. Be sarcastic. That'll make everything better."

Well, *something* had to. Nothing else was working.

Ryan linked his hands together on the paper place mat. "Get mad at me if you want to, but you know I'm right. A cop with un-resolved personal issues is dangerous. You've seen it before. Do whatever you have to so things can get back to normal. But do it fast because I'm not going to wait for-ever."

She clamped her mouth shut.

Sinking back in the chair, she turned her cup in a listless circle on the table. "I'll fix it."

"When?"

"Soon. Now." She lifted her gaze. "Right away." God only knew *how* she'd do it, but she couldn't lose her career. She'd already lost her family. The department was all she had left.

It was only later, as Jolene trailed Ryan back to the car, that she realized she'd left out one important piece of information. She hadn't told him she was part Cherokee, and couldn't honestly say whether it had been by accident or design.

WHILE HIS SUNDAY MORNING coffee brewed, Mason attacked the kitchen floor with a broom. Warm spring sunlight streamed in through the open blinds, and the unopened Sunday edition of *Tulsa World* waited for him on the table.

It had been almost a week since Alexandra's phone call, and he still hadn't found the right way to tell Debra that her mother planned to leave her here longer than either of them had first thought. He wasn't even sure why he kept putting it off. He only knew that every time he tried to tell her, something kept his mouth shut. That had to change.

Alex would be calling later, and she would assume Mason had told Debra. If he had any hope of saving his relationship with the girl, he had to be honest with her. Letting her find out because Alex inadvertently let the news slip wasn't going to win any points with his daughter.

It would be so much easier to talk with her if they could just stop butting heads. It seemed that the more he tried to interact with her, the more petulant and surly she became. Take last night, for example. He hadn't bothered to rush home last night because he knew Debra would be at diving practice until six o'clock. By six-thirty he was in the kitchen and starting dinner, but that wasn't good enough for Debra. Without once giving him a clue about what he was doing wrong, she'd sat at the table for at least thirty minutes, sullenly watching him from the corner of her eye, her chin propped in one hand.

All those dreams he'd once had about fatherhood sure didn't match the reality. The whole time Debra had been living with her mother, Mason had carried around images of what life would be like if only they could spend more time together. He'd conjured up walks through the park, visits to the zoo, movies, dinners and piggyback rides. A far cry from how they'd been living since the end of February.

Where were those dads whose daughters adored them? The daughters who thought their daddies could do no wrong? Or were they just another fairy tale?

As if he'd conjured her up, Debra shuffled into the kitchen, hair tousled, face still puffy from sleep. She went straight to the fridge, pulled out the milk and poured herself a tall glass.

Hardly the action of a kid on drugs—was it? He'd checked her eyes a hundred times in the past week, and every time they looked clear and bright, but would he ever really know for sure?

He dumped the dirt he'd swept up into the trash, then put the broom away. "Morning, kid. You're up early, aren't you?"

"Yeah. So? I have to get started on my history report."

She was going to do homework willingly? He couldn't ask for more than that. "I was just thinking about making chocolate chip pancakes. Sound good to you?"

Debra shrugged and dropped onto one of the chairs by the table. "I guess."

"What kind of fruit do you want with that?"

"I don't want fruit."

"You need to eat balanced meals, Debra, especially when you're in training. Coach wants you in good condition for the meet next week, and he's going to be doing trials tomorrow."

She kicked her feet onto a chair and slurped up a mouthful of milk. "I'm not going to practice tomorrow."

Mason should have known her attitude was too good to be true. He poured himself a coffee and carried it to the table. "You've already skipped too many practices," he said. "Do you have any idea how close you are to being kicked off the team?"

"So? I don't feel like going."

"Well, you can't just go through life doing only what you feel like doing. It doesn't work that way."

With an expressive roll of the eyes, Debra got up from the table and dug around in the cupboard for the chocolate powder. "I don't care about this team, so why should I care if I'm kicked off. It was your idea for me to be on it, not mine."

Mason sat across from the place she'd vacated. She wouldn't even let him do that. "I talked to Coach Walkenhorst about putting you on the team because your mother told me you loved diving at your other school."

"I did. This is different."

"So you want to quit because this coach does things a little differently from your last one? Or is it because you don't know the kids? There's only one way to change that."

She found the boxed powder and pulled it out of the cupboard. "I don't like the kids, I don't like the school, I don't like the coach and I don't like it *here*." She gestured broadly with one hand, hit her glass and sent it crashing to the floor. It shattered and milk splashed everywhere. She stared, but made no move to clean it up. "I want to go back home."

"This *is* home," Mason said, trying not to let her see how much that hurt. If she knew how steep her advantage was over him, he'd never be able to reach her. "It's home for a while longer, anyway, so it's time you started acting like it. You can begin by cleaning up the mess you just made."

Debra glared at him. "Why?"

"Why do you have to clean up the mess?"

"No, why does this have to be home? It's not like you want me here, and Mom said I wouldn't have to stay if I didn't like it."

"Hold on a second, Debra. What makes you think I don't want you here?"

"You don't."

"Of course I do."

"I'm only here because she made you take me."

"That's not true. Your mother called me, but she didn't *make* me do anything. I wanted you to come and stay with me, I just didn't think you'd want to."

"Well, you were right."

Her words stung, but the look on her face brought back memories from his own childhood and saddened him. "Listen, Deb, I know I haven't always been the best dad around. I even understand why you feel the way you do. But I *do* love you. I just wish I could find some way to make you believe that."

"You could help me with my report."

Mason started to agree, realized she was talking about *that* report and froze. "The one about your grandparents?"

"How do you know about it?"

"Your mother told me, but there's no way you can interview either of my parents, Debra. My mother's been dead for more than twenty-five years."

She clucked her tongue against her teeth. "Well, duh. I know that."

"And I haven't seen my father since I was ten."

"But that's okay because Mr. Hopewell said I could do a different kind of report if you'd help me with it. All he wants us to do is learn about our personal history, so if you'll just answer questions, I can still do the report."

The blood moved through his veins like sludge. "What kind of questions?"

"Just stuff about your mom and dad,

maybe about Henry. And about, you know, the Cherokee."

"Grandpa Hicks worked for the government for a long time, you know. He'd be really interesting to interview."

Debra's mouth thinned with disgust at his predictable response. "I don't want to interview Grandpa Hicks. I want to know about the rest of my family. The family you never, ever talk about."

"I have good reason."

"But they're *my* grandparents."

Mason fought to keep from raising his voice. "You have no idea what kind of people they were, and I don't want you to know. Bad enough they messed up my life. I don't want them doing the same to you."

"That's stupid, Dad. How can they if they're not even around?"

"Knowing those two, easily." He abandoned his coffee and got up to start making pancakes. "You're not going to do your report on my parents, Debra. Find another subject."

"Okay. Henry."

"We weren't even related. How will that count?"

"If he raised you, then he's part of my

past. So tell me about Henry and what he taught you."

Mason pulled pancake mix from the cupboard along with a bag of chocolate chips. "Why do you want to hear about a bunch of old legends?"

"Because my ancestors believed them."

"For all the good that did them. Trust me, kiddo, the best way to get anywhere in this life is to leave old superstitions in the past where they belong. None of it did a bit of good for the Cherokee forced to walk the Trail of Tears in the eighteen hundreds. And it didn't do anything for my parents, either."

Debra's eyes lit up. "Did they believe in it?"

"Who? My parents?" Mason snorted. "My dad didn't believe in anything. But my mother couldn't get enough. She'd sit around for hours, doing nothing but reading." *And drinking*.

"And that's why you hate it all?"

He'd stop right there, except that Debra was talking to him—*really* talking to him. For the first time since she came to Tulsa. "Hate's a pretty strong word," he said, gripping the counter with both hands. "It's probably better to say that I resent it. A lot."

"Why?"

"I guess the best way to describe my mother is to say that she liked playing the victim, and she never had any trouble finding something to blame for her hard luck. I was just a little kid when she latched on to Cherokee history as her favorite scapegoat, and she spent the rest of her life blaming white people for her misery."

"She hated white people?"

"She blamed them for the fact that she couldn't hold down a job and we never had any money. She'd complain about how much better our lives would have been if the government hadn't forced us to relocate here."

"Well, it *wasn't* fair," Debra said. "They shouldn't have been able to do that."

"I never said it was fair or that it was right. But it happened a hundred and seventy years ago. At some point, you've got to stop blaming that for the choices you make today."

"Is that why you hate her?"

How was he supposed to answer that? That's why it's never a good idea to tell someone half of the story. But no way in hell he'd tell Debra the whole thing. He nodded and pulled a mixing bowl from the cupboard. "Yeah. That's why."

"No offense, Dad, but that's kind of lame."

"You think so?"

"Well, yeah. I mean, I'm not saying that what she did was good, but it's actually kind of pathetic, don't you think? You should feel sorry for her."

That's what Henry had always told him, too. But why should he, when she'd done such a bang-up job of feeling sorry for herself? And now she had Debra's sympathy, as well. Next time she asked about his family, he'd be smart enough to keep his big mouth shut.

CHAPTER TWELVE

TWO WEEKS AFTER Ryan had issued his ultimatum at the Blue Plate, Jolene was no closer to working through her personal issues. Not that she'd had time.

Thanks to the department's staff shortage they'd all been putting in extra hours. Tempers were flaring all over the building, and everyone was looking for someone to blame when things went wrong. Raoul Zika continued to slither out of their grasp every time they turned around.

Just before their shift ended on Saturday night, Ryan and Jolene picked up a lead on someone who might know where Big Red was—a hairdresser named Vivienne Beck. First thing Tuesday morning, they planned to track her down.

Meanwhile, Jolene finally had a couple of days off, so she hit the sack early, hoping that a good night's sleep would help her put her personal life back together. Unfortunately, it wasn't so easy to actually *get* to sleep. A storm blew in during the night, and the sound of raindrops on the pavement outside her window didn't soothe her the way it usually did. She lay awake far into the night, longing for the warmth and security she'd had for the first thirty years of her life, and wondering if she'd ever know anything like it again.

It was nearly four o'clock when she finally gave up trying to sleep and climbed out of bed. If she couldn't rest, then she ought to be doing something useful, like tackling the housework she'd left for far too long. Since moving into this apartment, she'd been home just long enough to make a mess, never long enough to clean it up.

After throwing on a pair of faded jeans and an old T-shirt, she unpacked three boxes of books, found the extra bedding she'd been missing since the move, and her screwdriver and pliers. As the sky lightened, she broke down the boxes and made a mad dash to the trash, slowing just long enough to check out Mason's apartment as she passed.

Still dark. That figured. Only bakers, milkmen, drug addicts and cops were awake at this time of the morning. Normal people—like Mason—were still sound asleep.

It had been years since she'd thought about the possibility of a regular life. Home. Kids. Husband. Dog. To tell the truth, she'd given up on it. At least she thought she had.

She stuffed sodden cardboard into the overflowing trash barrel and wondered how other cops did it. How did Ryan go home to his wife and kids with the stink of that rat-infested sinkhole on his clothes? How did Captain Eisley bounce grandkids on his knee after watching some junkie die from an overdose? Maybe they had an emotional switch she didn't have. Or maybe she just didn't know how to flip it.

She jogged across the rain-soaked lawn. Listen to her! She'd felt excited when she looked at Mason, and now her imagination was running wild. All it had taken was a little interest on his part. But with Debra fighting him at every turn, his life wasn't in much better shape than Jolene's was. So yeah, there'd been a spark there, but neither of them could look away long enough to see where it might go.

Not that it mattered. Her love life had been a complete disaster for years, populated by way too many brief encounters. The closest she'd come to the real thing was Kevin Webber in her junior year of college, and that had only lasted six months. Not exactly an impressive romantic résumé.

She glanced at Mason's windows once more before rounding the corner. A light had come on. So he was an early riser, huh?

Turning resolutely toward home, she told herself to get a grip. This wasn't about Mason, it was about her and her need for emotional security. Her longing for something that made sense and someone who made her feel wanted. It was about the empty place where her family used to be, nothing more, nothing less. Mason and Debra had enough on their plates. Neither of them needed to be used as a substitute for something else.

She spent the next two hours straightening the living room, removing the film of dust from the furniture and washing and folding three batches of laundry. With that done, she scrubbed kitchen counters and mopped the kitchen and bathroom floors, then finally stripped out of her old clothes and jumped into the shower.

But the physical exertion hadn't done anything to slow the questions racing through her head. She stood under the spray for a long time, letting the pulse of the water drum away some of the tension in her neck and shoulders, then finally, before the hot water ran out, scrubbing herself clean and washing her hair.

Think. Pretend this was someone else's problem. What would she advise them to do?

According to Lawrence Preston, the first step in solving any problem was to find out everything you could about it. *Break it down, Jolene.*

What did that mean in her case?

Avoiding the issue wasn't working, so she needed to change tactics. Tackle the problem head-on. First, she needed to learn everything she could about the culture she came from. Second, when she was ready, she'd have to learn everything she could about the family she'd never met. And third?

The third step, she supposed, would be to meet them.

Step one. That's all she had to think about for the moment. She could visit the Cherokee Cultural Center, but even that felt like too much of a commitment. She could research on the Internet, but how would she know the good sites from those riddled with inaccuracies? Finally, giving in to Lawrence's influence, she decided that the most logical place to begin was the library.

Taking advantage of her day off, she dressed in a pair of black slacks and a comfortable red sweater she'd had for years. On impulse, she changed the gold posts she usually wore in her ears to a pair of red earrings her aunt Chloe had given her for Christmas.

As she did every morning of her life, she reached for her brush and a band so she could pull her hair into a pony tail, but this morning something made her stop. It had been a long time since she'd spent this much time getting ready for anything, and even longer since she'd taken a good, long look in the mirror. Whether she wanted to admit it or not, meeting Mason had made her more aware of herself than she'd been in a long, long time.

Carefully setting the brush aside, she studied her reflection, searching every feature, comparing what she really saw to what she'd always assumed about herself.

She'd spent most of her adult life not really caring about her appearance. Now she wondered what other people saw when they looked at her. Ryan saw her as one of the guys, but she'd worked long and hard to make sure he did. But what about other people, like Mason for instance? What did he see?

Long hair. Straight, dark brown hair. One dark head in a family of blondes. And her eyes. Hers were the only dark brown eyes in the lot. A few people had commented on how different she looked from the rest of her family, but someone had told her once that she was a throwback to a previous generation, and she'd believed it. There'd been no reason not to. She'd believed in who she was.

Even as she told herself that, she knew it wasn't true. She'd never felt completely secure. She'd been a tomboy in a family of academics, the child whose likes and dislikes had confused her parents since her earliest memory. At least Jolene had assumed they'd been confused. Now she realized that they'd probably been terrified that she would stumble across the truth.

What she needed was something solid to ground her—something she knew to be true about herself that could serve as a foundation for rebuilding her life. But there was nothing. Not one thing she could say with absolute certainty was real.

She grabbed her keys and wallet and headed into the parking lot. A breeze rustled the budding leaves in the trees and the scent of freshly dug earth made everything seem fresh and new. She took a deep breath and turned her face to the sun, relishing its warmth on her skin. There had to be answers she could live with. But she wasn't going to find them by staring in the mirror.

In spite of the warm spring weather, the drive to the library seemed endless. Traffic was heavy and snarled in almost every direction by closures from road construction. By the time she pulled into the library's small, crowded parking lot her already frayed nerves felt as though someone had set a match to them.

She was about halfway to the building when she heard someone call her name. Half-convinced that she'd imagined it, she glanced over her shoulder and saw Mason jogging up the sidewalk behind her.

Sure enough, she felt that tingle of awareness and was inordinately pleased with herself for going to all the trouble to dress up.

"I thought that was you," he said, panting slightly. "What are you doing here?"

His eyes darkened as they traveled along her sweater, the length of her legs, and slowly, slowly back up to her face.

She caught her breath and her pulse sped to an unsteady rhythm she tried to ignore. Getting all hot and bothered over Mason couldn't possibly make her life better. "I came to do some research," she said, casually assessing the deep brown of his eyes and the way the sun found golden highlights in his dark hair. "What about you?"

"Same." They fell into step as if strolling along the sidewalk together were the most natural thing in the world. "Debra's doing a report for history, and I thought I'd pick up a couple of books that might help her."

"That's nice of you. My dad would have made me find the books myself."

"Yeah? Well, what can I say? I'm a swell guy." He grinned and she wished he'd do that more often. "What are you researching?"

Good question. What was she researching? She didn't even know enough to have questions. "Actually, I'm looking for some basic information on the Cherokee. Any suggestions?"

Did she only imagine it, or did Mason's step falter? If it did, he recovered smoothly. "Does this have anything to do with the former Margaret Starr?"

Her first instinct was to say no, but how would that help? She made herself nod. "Yes, it does." But that was only partially true. Taking a deep breath, she said, "What I'd like even more than research material is for you to tell me everything you know about Billy Starr."

Mason nodded as if people asked him about Billy Starr every day of the week. "What do you want to know?"

Jolene's next question was a little easier to ask. "What kind of man was he?"

"I don't know a lot about him, but I'd say he was interested in his heritage. Must have been to spend so much time starting the Cultural Center."

"Does he have family around here?"

Mason slowed his pace. "Yes, but if you're going to ask about people who are still alive, you're going to have to tell me why you want to know. Is this a police matter?"

She shook her head quickly. "No."

"But it has something to do with his wife."

She nodded again. "With the woman in the article, yes."

"Who is she? A friend of yours?"

Why was it so hard to tell him? What was wrong with her? Slowly, she met his gaze. "Don't make me answer that yet."

"You don't have to tell me anything you don't want to," Mason said with a casual shrug, "but I reserve the same right. If you want answers from me, you're going to have to give a few."

She couldn't argue with that. Fair was fair. "Would it make any difference if I told you that I'm part Cherokee?"

"You?" Mason studied her face but she

couldn't tell whether he was pleased or disgusted. "Why didn't you say something before?"

"Because I didn't know until recently."

"Let me guess—you found a long-lost Cherokee princess on your family tree."

"You really shouldn't say something that stupid to a woman with a gun.

He managed to look a little sheepish. "I apologize. No Cherokee princess."

"Nope."

"Okay, then, fill in the blanks for me. How did you find out you're part Cherokee?"

"I mentioned that article I found at your place to my mother. She reminded me of the woman in the photograph, and I thought it was an interesting coincidence."

"Are you telling me your mother is Margaret Starr?"

"She was." Jolene pressed her fingertips to her eyes. "I had no idea. I just thought it was odd that Margaret Starr looked so much like her. I didn't even know my mother had been married before. It was quite a shock. I'm sure you can imagine."

"I'll bet it was. And not a pleasant one, either, judging from the look on your face."

"You're right about that."

"Does that mean you're Billy Starr's daughter?"

"So I'm told."

Mason whistled softly. "Well, I'll be damned. So what do you want from me?"

"I don't want anything. I'm still trying to figure out how I feel about it."

"About being Cherokee?"

"About *not* being who I thought I was. Race has nothing to do with it, if that's what you're wondering."

Mason pretended to believe her, but even she knew that her protest hadn't rung quite true. "So why don't you just contact Billy's family and ask?"

Jolene shook her head quickly. "I'm not ready for them to know about me yet."

"You're not going to tell them?"

"Someday. I just don't know when. In the meantime, I'm just trying to keep breathing. I'm not trying to hurt anybody, Mason."

Mason stuffed his hands into his pockets and tilted his head to the sky.

Suddenly, it seemed very important that he agree to help her. She knew Mason had negative feelings about his heritage, but that meant he wouldn't push her into anything. The perfect resource.

"So what do you want to know?"

She breathed a sigh of relief. "I wish I could answer that. All I know is I have to figure this out. Decide who I am again. Figure out how I feel about that, and get back to normal—whatever that is—before my partner convinces my captain that I'm a risk to the other guys in the squad. The captain would use this as an excuse to transfer me out."

Mason's eyebrow arched. "He's looking for one?"

"I'm a woman doing a 'man's job.' Some guys can handle it. Some can't. My captain thinks I'm emotional and unfocused. Too busy thinking about fashion and babies, I guess."

Mason raked a gaze across her face that left her distinctly uncomfortable. "You don't want kids?"

"I don't have anything against kids," she assured him quickly, "and I don't *not* want them. When I was younger, I always thought I'd have one or two, but it didn't happen, and now… Well, now I don't see them in my future, that's all. Men on the force can have a home and family and get away with it. It's harder for women."

"It shouldn't be."

"But it is. If life were the way it *should* be, a whole lot of things would be different."

Mason conceded that point with a dip of his head. "So your job is on the line if you don't pull all of this together in some way you can live with? Well, good. There's no pressure, then."

Jolene grinned. "I'm not asking you to work miracles," she assured him. "Just tell me what to read. Answer questions. I know how you feel about your heritage, and I know it's a lot to ask…"

He leaned against a support post and shook his head. "Have you ever felt as if everything is conspiring to make you do something? Something you really don't want to do?" When Jolene didn't respond, he gave a hollow laugh. "First Debra, and now you. I guess it's time for me to deal with my past."

Jolene held up both hands. "I don't want you to do anything that makes you uncomfortable."

"Everything about this is going to make me uncomfortable," he said, shoving away from the post. "But I have it on good authority that I'm pretty lame, so what's a guy to do, huh? Ike tells me there's a powwow coming up in a couple of weeks. You might want to start by checking that out."

"A powwow?" she asked, touched that he would put Debra first and hoping her voice sounded reasonably normal. "They still have those?"

"All the time. The one Ike told me about is being sponsored by the Cherokee Cultural Center to raise money for the tribal elders. I'm probably going to have to take Debra. Are you interested in joining us?"

Jolene nodded. "Yes. Thanks. But are you sure you're okay with all of this?"

"No. But I'll survive." He stepped past her and opened the library's heavy glass door. "Ready? I'll show you some books that will get you started."

She stepped through the door, more aware of him than ever, of his height, the slightly spicy scent of his aftershave, the cut of his jaw and the steely determination in his eye. But this was so much more than the physical attraction that had been nagging at her since the day they met, and she had a feeling this wasn't going to be easy to ignore.

CHAPTER THIRTEEN

THE NEXT FEW DAYS FLEW by so quickly,
Jolene barely had time to think. Increased
activity on their beat gave evidence of a new
meth lab in the area. Mike Santini and his
partner, Darren Ross, made an arrest just ten
feet from an elementary school, and the
dealer they hauled in—a registered sex
offender known to target six- to eight-year-
olds—gave everyone on the squad the creeps.
It was Friday before Jolene and Ryan had a
chance to track down their lead on Vivienne
Beck.

They found Vivienne working at The
Beauty Mark on 11th Street, a low-slung
concrete block building that spewed noxious
chemical scents every time the door opened.
How some women could subject themselves
to hours of poking, prodding, pulling, yank-
ing, waxing, filing and lacquering was

beyond Jolene's comprehension. The twenty minutes she spent having her hair trimmed once every three months was almost more than she could tolerate.

As they approached the salon, the door opened and two Latino women deep in conversation came out. Each clutched a collection of bags from a morning shopping expedition, both wore formfitting pants and camisoles edged with lace and beads. In spite of her aversion to the whole beauty and fashion thing, Jolene suddenly felt large and clumsy in her industrial-strength slacks, toss-it-in-the-washer blazer and sensible flat-soled shoes.

Ryan's head turned briefly as the women passed, and Jolene found herself wondering what it felt like to be that kind of woman. Not that she wanted to be. Not really. Although it might be nice to know you could turn *one* man's head.

She took one last breath of fresh air and ducked through the door. Alan Jackson's "Chatahoochie" played softly in the background, but the women inside were all too busy to pay attention.

Since Ryan seemed convinced that they

were wasting their time, Jolene took the lead. They were directed to the back of the salon by a skunk-haired receptionist who told them Vivienne was folding towels in the employee break room.

Sure enough, they found a small woman with spiky hair so dark it was almost black working on the towels, clearly bored. Beneath her black smock, she wore a short skirt and her bare feet were arched into stiletto heels so high Jolene's calf muscles cramped in sympathy.

The woman, who Jolene guessed to be in her midtwenties, glanced up when she sensed movement by the door. Seeing them, she frowned. Before Jolene could even open her mouth, though, she slumped against the wall. "Don't tell me—cops, right?"

Jolene nodded and moved into the room. The homey scent of fabric softener took the burn out of the chemical-laced air. "That's right. Are you Vivienne Beck?"

"I am." She got up to put a stack of towels in an overhead cupboard. The hem of her skirt drooped in the back where the stitching had come undone, but either she didn't know or she didn't care. "What do you want?"

"I'm Sergeant Preston, with Tulsa PD. This is my partner Detective Fielding. We'd like to ask you a few questions, if you don't mind."

Vivienne regarded them through close-set blue eyes, their color startling and unnatural in contrast to her nearly black hair. "About what?"

"We're looking for a guy who goes by the name of Big Red. We were told you might know where to find him."

Vivienne rolled her eyes and shut the cupboard with a bang. "Surprise, surprise. Red's having trouble with the police." Returning to the table, she swept something onto the floor and picked up a second stack of towels. "How'd you find me?"

"Someone mentioned your name. Do you know where we can find Red?"

"No. Sorry."

Ryan looked smug, but Jolene thought it was a predictable answer. Nobody ever knows where to find anybody else—at least not the first few times they're asked. "Can you tell us when you saw him last?"

Vivienne shrugged and pulled a fresh load of towels from the dryer. "A few weeks ago, maybe."

"Are you planning on seeing him again soon?"

"I never plan on anything when it comes to Red," Vivienne said, her voice suddenly sharp. "He comes and goes. I never know when he's going to be around and when he isn't."

Trying to look like someone Vivienne could confide in, Jolene worked up a sympathetic smile. "That must drive you crazy."

"Not really. You get used to it."

"Yeah, I guess you would. So the two of you haven't split up, then?"

"Split up?" Vivienne laughed through her nose. "You think Red is my boyfriend?"

"He's not?"

"No. He's my brother."

Jolene looked at Ryan, but his expression didn't change, didn't give anything away. "My mistake," she said with a smile. "Then you can tell us what his real name is, can't you?"

Vivienne shrugged. "Sure. Why not? It's Russell Alan Beck. Red to his friends. So tell me, what's he done now?"

Ryan answered while Jolene jotted down the information Vivienne had given them so far. "He hasn't done anything that we know of."

Vivienne looked confused, so Jolene offered a bit more. "Nobody's seen him for a couple of weeks. We're trying to make sure he's all right."

The young woman's expression clouded. "You *are* cops, aren't you?"

"Yes we are."

"And you just stopped by to make sure my junkie brother is all right? What is this, a slow crime day?"

"It's more complicated than that," Jolene admitted, "but we do need to find him. It's important."

"When you saw him last," Ryan said, "how did he seem to you?"

"Pretty much the same as always."

"He didn't seem worried? Agitated? Nervous?"

"No," Vivienne said slowly. "Why? Did something happen to him?"

Ryan ignored the question. "Did he say anything to you that might help us figure out where he is?"

"We didn't talk much. I don't have a lot to say to him." She looked from one to the other slowly, and Jolene could see the woman's irritation giving way to fear. "You think something's happened to him, don't you?"

Jolene tried not to compare her family situation with Vivienne's, but she knew that if anything happened to her parents or Trevor while they were estranged, she'd have to live with the guilt for the rest of her life. "We don't know," she reassured Vivienne. "We're trying to find out."

Clearly shaken, Vivienne sank onto a chair. "What do you think happened to him?"

"Maybe nothing," Jolene said before Ryan could answer. "It's possible he's just lying low somewhere."

"Hiding? Why? From what?"

"That's what we're trying to figure out. You said you saw him a few weeks ago?"

Vivienne nodded and drew a towel from the pile in front of her. "That's right."

"Do you remember the date?"

"The middle of April. Tax day."

The day after the failed Zika bust. Jolene leaned forward. Even Ryan looked interested in that. "You're sure about that?" he asked.

"Yeah. Positive. He ripped off the money my dad was going to pay his taxes with." She smiled halfheartedly. "He's bled my parents dry for years and ripped me off so many times I've lost count. He even stole from my grandmother while she was in bed dying of cancer. What kind of person does that?"

That was a question Jolene wouldn't answer. "Did he steal from you the last time you saw him?"

"Me? No. I've finally learned my lesson."

"Are you sure your parents didn't give the money to Red voluntarily?"

"Positive. I thought my dad was going to have a heart attack when they found out it was gone." Vivienne spotted a string dangling from a towel, wrapped it around her finger and snapped it off. "My parents don't have a lot. We're all doing good just to scrape by."

"How much did he take?" Ryan asked.

"A little over two thousand. He got my mother's ATM card. She's a... Well, she's always been softhearted when it comes to Red. Either she told him the PIN code or he guessed it. However he got it, he cleaned out her checking account, and nobody's seen him since."

Ryan met Jolene's gaze over Vivienne's head. "Two thousand wouldn't last long on the streets."

"That would depend on where he goes, wouldn't it?" Jolene asked. "Has he been in contact with either of your parents since then?"

"He's not stupid enough to contact my dad," Vivienne said with a humorless smile, "but I suppose he might have called Mom. She probably wouldn't tell me if he had."

Jolene added Mommy Dearest to the list of people she wanted to talk to. "Can you think of anywhere he might have gone if he wanted to lie low? Somewhere he might consider safe?"

Vivienne shook her head. "No, but then he disappears so often, I've given up trying to figure him out. We don't see him for weeks and even months at a time, but eventually he runs out of money and shows up again."

Ryan pulled a business card from his pocket and passed it to her. "I'm sure that's what's happened this time, too. Thank you for your time, Ms. Beck. If you think of anything else, give one of us a call."

Stunned by his sudden about-face, Jolene

trailed him through the salon. She held her tongue until they were outside on the sidewalk, but there she rounded on him. "What was that?"

Ryan stepped around her and started toward the car. "What was what?"

"That crap you just pulled inside. I wasn't finished with her."

"You're wasting your time, Jo. She doesn't know anything."

His attitude made her cheeks burn. "She knew Red found himself a nice little bankroll before he disappeared," she snapped. Ryan loped across the street during a break in traffic. Growing more furious by the second, Jolene followed and slid into the Crown Vic just as Ryan started the engine. "You're so determined to be right, you're not even listening."

Ryan pulled into traffic. "Getting emotional about this isn't going to help, Jo."

Jolene's mouth fell open. "Emotional? What the hell are you talking about?"

"Are you going to tell me you aren't letting Big Red's disappearance get to you?"

"What's getting to me," Jolene snarled, "is the way you don't seem to care. You've decided he's dead in some alley or under some bridge, and you'd rather not be bothered to look any further."

"He's been missing for three weeks," Ryan pointed out with annoying calm. "If he were still alive, he'd have surfaced already, if only to score a buy."

"Not if he has a good reason to stay hidden."

"He left his duffel bag behind. He never went anywhere without that thing."

"He stole two thousand dollars a couple of days before he disappeared, and there's no sign of that money in his pack."

"Which there wouldn't be if someone rolled him for the money."

"If someone rolled him for the money, we'd have a body, wouldn't we?" That shut Ryan up. "If Red wanted Raoul Zika to back off, appearing to disappear is one way to do it."

A scowl puckered Ryan's face as he stopped for a traffic light. "So now you think he faked his own death? Come on, Jo. Get real."

She shifted in her seat as far as her seat belt would allow. "Look, I know there's no evidence to support my theory. I *know* that.

It's just a feeling. You saw the look on Red's face when he was telling us about that shipment. He wasn't telling us everything he knew."

"That's pure speculation."

"Yeah, and so's this. We show up the night Zika's planning to move the drugs. He knows we're there because I roust the kids. But why do you think somebody like Red knew about that shipment in the first place? Why would Zika tell Red, of all people, that he's planning on moving a shipment of dope?"

Very slowly, Ryan shrugged. "He wouldn't."

"No, he wouldn't. My guess is that only a few trusted people knew about that shipment. But then we show up, and three days later, Red just happens to overdose or take a dive off a bridge. Coincidence?"

"Could be," Ryan said, but he didn't sound nearly so confident now.

"Could also be that Red wasn't supposed to know about that shipment. Maybe he was somewhere he shouldn't have been, heard something he shouldn't have heard and he saw it as a chance to improve his standard of living."

"By calling us?"

"Why not? He's facing drug charges that could put him away for a long time. He accidentally picks up a choice piece of information but, through no fault of his own, the bust that's supposed to earn his freedom goes sour. What does he do next?"

Ryan took his eyes off the road for a heartbeat. "You think he went to Zika?"

"No, I don't think Red is that stupid. But I think he told someone else, and I think whoever he told ratted him out. Somehow, he found out and went into hiding."

"That's where your theory really falls apart," Ryan said. "Red didn't know anything that posed a threat to Zika. The bust—as you said—went sour. Zika was in the clear."

"Which brings us right back to my idea that Red knew more than what he told us."

Ryan thought about that for a couple of blocks. "Even if you're right," he said at last, "that backs up my theory as much as it does yours. Red has something on Zika. Zika finds out, and—" He put two fingers to his forehead and pretended to pull the trigger.

"But it also means that if Red *is* dead, it wasn't an accident."

Ryan shook his head firmly. "It's an interesting theory, but there's still not one shred of evidence to support it."

"That's because we haven't been asking the right questions. I think we should talk to OC again. I'll bet anything that OC is either the one who ratted Red out to Zika, or he knows who did."

"And if you're wrong?"

"Then I'm wrong. No big deal."

"You sure about that?"

"Of course I'm sure. Why wouldn't I be?"

Ryan looked at the passing storefronts for half a block or so then said, "I think you're blaming yourself for Red's disappearance. That's why you're grasping at solutions, even when they don't make a whole lot of sense, and that's why you're so determined to see this through."

"You're wrong."

"Am I?" He glanced at her.

"Absolutely. I'm just trying to do my job."

"By making sure you don't shoulder the blame. Red gave us a tip. Now he's gone, and you're trying to make sure nobody can blame you for that."

She stared at him in disbelief. "Are you

crazy? Why would I even think someone might blame me?"

"Because we would have had Zika if not for those kids."

Jolene began to feel uneasy. "Do you really believe that?"

"You don't?"

"Now which one of us is delusional?" she asked, trying to sound more confident than she felt. "Zika has slipped through our fingers several times. What makes you think this bust would have been any different?"

He shrugged. "I guess we'll never know, will we?"

No. They wouldn't. She hadn't thought of the search for Big Red as personal before, but if the guys in the squad were joining Eisley in blaming her for the failure to bag Zika, it was definitely personal now.

She refused to even think about what might happen to her career if they couldn't find him.

CHAPTER FOURTEEN

MASON PLANTED HIS SHOVEL in the soft earth at his feet and reached for the water bottle he'd left sitting nearby. The sun hadn't climbed very high in the sky and a cool spring breeze rustled the leaves, but he'd managed to work up a healthy sweat digging compost into the tight clay soil.

He didn't mind physical exertion. In fact, he'd always found it easier to think through a problem when he was doing some kind of manual labor.

He'd finally told Debra that she'd be staying in Tulsa for another six months, but since then her disposition had grown even more volatile and she'd skipped so many diving practices, her position on the team was hanging by a thread. Mason had given her the books he'd picked up at the library, but he didn't think she'd even opened them yet. She still wanted him to spill his guts about his childhood.

When he wasn't worrying about Debra, his thoughts strayed to Jolene, and that was another problem entirely. He could be loading the dishwasher, folding towels, studying landscape plans for the county project, talking to a potential new client, calculating payroll—it didn't matter where he was or what he was doing, suddenly he'd be thinking about the warmth in her voice, the citrus scent of her shampoo or the intelligence in her eyes.

Their schedules had kept them apart all week, but they'd made plans to get together tonight over pizza. Knowing that he'd see her that evening had distracted him all morning, and he was anticipating the evening, even if he'd have to spend it talking about things he'd rather not.

It took a whole lot of effort to pull his thoughts back to the job. According to the schedule he'd given the county commissioners, this row of bald cypress trees should have been planted three days ago, but too many factors had conspired to work against them over the past few weeks, starting with

missing shipments of plants and ending with
the loss of two crew members.

Mason had always been a hands-on boss,
determined not to ask his crew to do
anything he wouldn't do himself. That
meant long hours most days and overtime on
the weekends. Working twelve-hour days
had never bothered him before. In fact,
they'd been proof that he wasn't turning into
his own father—a shiftless loser who'd
drifted from bottle to bottle and woman to
woman in search of an easy way out. But
now that Debra was here, the guilt over
being away from home so much was starting
to take its toll. More and more he found
himself wondering where to draw the line.

He glanced over his shoulder at the three
men digging behind him and gauged their
progress. After the bald cypress were in the
ground, they still had a shipment of sum-
mer-flowering bulbs to plant before they
were ready for the shipment of annuals
coming tomorrow. Even if everything went
like clockwork today, they'd be hard-pressed
to get back on schedule.

Tossing aside the water bottle, he reached
for the shovel again when his cell phone rang

for what felt like the hundredth time. Annoyed by the interruption, he pulled out the phone and answered without even looking at the caller ID. "Blackfox Landscape."

"Is Mr. Blackfox in?" The female voice was unfamiliar.

"You've got him. How can I help you?"

"This is Shirley Carmichael, secretary at Edison Middle School. Mr. Davies, the school principal, asked me to call. He'd like to meet with you this afternoon if it's convenient."

This wasn't the first time he'd been called by someone at Debra's school, and he wondered what new crisis was on the horizon. More missing textbooks? Another unpaid locker fee? Had he topped off her lunch money account recently? "Today? That's kind of short notice, isn't it?"

"Yes, and I apologize. But it's important. He wouldn't ask, otherwise."

Mason tugged off one work glove and brushed a clump of dirt from his knee. "Is this something we can handle over the phone? I have a very tight schedule today."

"I'm afraid not. There's been an incident involving Debra."

"What kind of incident? Is she hurt?"

"Debra is fine," the secretary assured him. "It's just that some items of concern were discovered in her locker today during a routine search."

Mason could have sworn the ground beneath his feet disappeared. "What exactly are 'items of concern'?"

"I think Mr. Davies would like to explain that when he sees you."

"And I'd like you to tell me right now. What did you find in Debra's locker?"

The secretary took a deep breath, then gave him the list in a rush. "A baby's pacifier, several sets of colorful beads and a cigarette lighter."

"And those are a problem?"

"Well…yes."

"You want to explain why? I can't imagine what Debra's doing with a pacifier, but far as I know there's no law against having one, even if you're twelve."

"Admittedly, none of the items seems like much taken on its own, but together they form a pattern that concerns us all."

Was the woman purposely trying to drive him crazy? Or was he just being especially dense? "What kind of pattern?"

"I really think it would be best if Mr. Davies explained the rest."

"Look, lady, I don't want to sound rude, and I don't want to sound unconcerned about my daughter, but I'm not just sitting around home waiting for you to call. I'm up to my neck in work, and I'm not leaving here to drive all the way across town unless it's something I can't handle from here. I think it would be best if you just tell me now."

She hesitated for a moment, then sighed heavily. "Fine. I guess there's no easy way to say this. The school safety officer is afraid Debra is involved with drugs."

The shovel slipped out of Mason's hand and he came damn close to dropping the phone. "She's been using drugs at school?"

"We don't know that yet. The school district will require a test to determine that."

The knot of tension shifted to his neck. His kid undergoing a drug test? What if she wasn't using drugs? How traumatic would this be for her?

"Will you be able to come in and talk with Mr. Davies today?" the secretary asked again. "I'm sure he'll have more answers than I do."

Grim-faced, Mason cleared his throat. "I'll be there."

"Good. I'll let him know. Just check in with the office."

"Where is Debra now?"

"She's in her counselor's office. We'll keep her there until you're ready to take her home."

Home. What in the hell would he do with her then? What would he say to her? Irrationally wishing that he'd never answered, he disconnected and stuffed the phone back into his pocket and shouted for Schweppe to walk with him to his car.

All he'd ever wanted was order in his life. Sanity. A feeling of normalcy. It seemed little enough to ask for after the chaos of his childhood—an experience he'd never wanted to create for his own kid. But it seemed that every time he took one step forward, he ended up taking two steps back, and he felt further from sanity and order right this minute than he'd ever been.

HE MADE IT TO THE SCHOOL in record time and was immediately led by a red-haired secretary into the principal's large office. Mr. Davies, a tall man with rigid posture, stood as he entered, shook hands and motioned him to a chair. "Thank you for coming, Mr. Blackfox."

Mason didn't want to waste time on small talk. "What's going on here? What did you find in Debra's locker, and why were you looking for it?"

"It was a routine locker check," Mr. Davies explained. "We had no reason to suspect Debra was doing anything wrong. I want to make that perfectly clear. Once each month, our school officer and administrators do a random check of a dozen lockers. This month, we happened to draw Debra's number out of the hat."

"And this stuff you found. What was it again?"

"A baby pacifier hooked to her backpack. A collection of colorful plastic beads—" Mr. Davies reached behind him and produced the evidence "—and a lighter. As you can see, there's nothing inherently worrisome here, but grouped together, they form a pattern than sets off a warning."

"What about this makes you think my daughter is doing drugs?"

"The beads aren't used to actually take

drugs, but kids wear them at raves, and they're a big part of the culture. As for the pacifier, people who use ecstasy carry them because the drug makes them clench their teeth. Chewing on a pacifier softens the bite a little."

"Ecstasy?" Mason sank back in his chair. Three weeks ago, he'd been worried that she'd tried marijuana for the first time.

"If it helps," the principal said, "I don't think Debra actually did anything wrong. I think she's just confused and suffering from peer pressure. She's still not completely settled into the school and, according to her teachers, she hasn't really found a close group of friends. She's searching, I think. Trying to figure out where she fits."

"She's looking in the wrong place," Mason growled. "So what happens now? Your secretary mentioned that she'd have to pass a drug test. Is that it?"

"Unfortunately, no." Mr. Davies fixed Mason with a sympathetic look. "There's a required suspension that comes with pos-session of drug paraphernalia, Mr. Blackfox. That's mandated by the school district and out of my hands."

"Suspension?" Mason watched his orderly life slip further out of his grasp. "For how long?"

"No less than three days, maybe longer."

If Debra wasn't doing drugs, three days would feel like a lifetime. If she was, three days wasn't nearly long enough to straighten her out. And from a strictly practical standpoint, what would he do with a bored and sullen Debra on his hands for three days or more? He'd either have to leave her home alone while he worked, or he'd have to take an unplanned vacation. "You're going to kick her out of school for having a baby pacifier? If I didn't know these things were drug-related, what makes you think she knew?"

"She knew, Mr. Blackfox. The vice-principal warned several girls about the items just last week. Debra was one of them. As for the suspension, the timing of that is up to the district. If at the end of the required time a drug test comes back clean, Debra can return to class. She'll have to leave the diving team, though. At least until the end of this semester."

Mason stared at him, struggling to process

everything he was hearing. "But diving is all she has," he said, completely disregarding all the arguments Debra had been giving him against it. "If she hasn't actually taken any drugs, why can't she stay on the team?"

"Because she has the paraphernalia. I'm afraid this is bigger than Debra. We need to send a message to the entire student body."

"Using my daughter to do it." Mason's temper flared. "This isn't bigger than Debra, this *is* Debra. You're going to take away the one place where she fits in because she made a stupid decision trying to fit in? What sense does that make?"

Mr. Davies scowled his disapproval. "I understand how you feel, but I have nearly eight hundred students in this school, and only one set of rules. From that, I have to keep the students in line and the school functioning. I can't tailor the rules to fit the individual. If I did that we'd have pandemonium."

"But you're going to take away the one place where my kid has order in her life. You're practically guaranteeing that she'll fail."

The principal's stare was devoid of emotion. "Then I suggest you work closely with her while she's home to make sure that doesn't happen."

"Yeah. Well. The point is that leaving her home alone all day while I work isn't going to help her."

"Isn't there someone she can stay with? A family member? A friend?"

"No. I'm it. I'm all she has." The reality of that hit him full force.

Mr. Davies linked his hands together on the gleaming desk. "You seem like a caring father, Mr. Blackfox, and an intelligent man. I'm sure you'll figure it out. You'll need to meet with the administrators at the district level, and they may want a counselor to chat with Debra. We'll be in contact over the details. And now, unless you have further questions, I'll ask Mrs. Carmichael to bring Debra out."

Further questions? Mason had a million of 'em, but it was damn clear he wasn't going to find even one of the answers here. Obviously Debra had issues, but how could he help her if she wouldn't tell him what they were?

CHAPTER FIFTEEN

MASON WAS NO CLOSER to finding the answers by the time Jolene rang their doorbell than he'd been when he walked out of the school's front doors. Debra had spent most of the afternoon in her bedroom, blasting music loud enough to scrape paint off the walls while he tried to rearrange his schedule so he could be home with her during her suspension.

To his amazement, Debra's attitude shifted abruptly when Jolene arrived, and he stood just inside the kitchen doorway looking at them and wondering how getting along with Debra looked so effortless for Jolene. He hated the envy that took root as he watched. He should be grateful that Debra would at least talk to *somebody*.

He just couldn't stop wishing that somebody could've been him.

Later, when the only thing left of the gut-buster pizza he'd ordered were a couple of half-eaten crusts, and Debra had closeted herself in her bedroom with the library books—under protest—he spent five minutes dumping the garbage and loading the plates in the dishwasher, before carrying two glasses of iced tea into the living room. Jolene sat on the couch, shoes off, feet curled beneath her as she leafed through one of the old photo albums Henry had put together.

It was nothing fancy—just a few pictures stuck beneath self-adhesive plastic coating—but she seemed enthralled. If Jolene had an opinion about the absence of birth announcements and baby pictures, she didn't share it.

She looked up as he came toward her, a smile playing across her lips, her dark eyes luminous. He knew she was expecting him to help her make sense of her life, and he wanted to. He just didn't know how.

He handed her a glass and sat beside her, far more aware of her subtle scent and the warmth of her thigh where it touched his than he wanted to be. She must have noticed the contact, but either she didn't feel anything or she was a whole lot better at hiding it than he was.

"Tea?" she asked with a raised eyebrow.

"I'd offer you wine, but I don't drink."

"Okay. Tea's fine." She met his gaze over the rim of her glass. "I wish you'd let me help clean up."

"I had to throw away a cardboard box," Mason said, settling back in his corner of the couch. "There's really no way to split that job up."

She grinned and glanced toward the bedroom doors. "I didn't want to ask during dinner, but how's Debra doing? Any more trouble?"

Mason's smile faded. He'd half expected Debra to come clean about her trouble at school while they ate, but she'd skillfully avoided any mention of it. Maybe she didn't want Jolene to know, but Mason could use the benefit of her expertise. "She was suspended from school today for having drug paraphernalia," he said. "We're both a little edgy."

Jolene's lips thinned and right in front of his eyes she turned into the cop he'd met that first night. "What did she have?"

Holding up one finger, Mason retrieved the items from the kitchen cupboard where he'd put them. "I talked to the principal. He tells me they're relatively harmless, as paraphernalia goes."

Jolene's smile softened her features once more. "He's right. It's certainly not definitive proof she's using drugs."

He leaned forward, elbows on his knees and rubbed his face. "I feel like I'm watching her start to self-destruct. I know I should do something, but how do you stop something like this from happening?"

"If there were an easy answer, the world would be a far different place."

Not for the first time since he left the school, Mason's self-doubts overwhelmed him. "She shouldn't be here. She should be with her mother."

Jolene picked up one strand of beads and studied them thoughtfully. "I'm not so sure about that. If her mother's focused on her new husband and their marriage, this might actually be a better place for Debra while she's going through this."

"She probably wouldn't be going through it if she were home."

"Stop selling yourself short. It's not your fault Debra's making these choices."

Oh, if she only knew.

"You're a good dad," Jolene assured him. "Trust your instincts with her."

"I'm not sure I have any instincts."

"You had a great role model in Henry. Look how well you turned out."

He almost laughed at that. "Yeah. Henry." Who almost made up for his father.

Jolene looked away, and he had the sense that she was giving him time to compose himself. After a few minutes she ran her fingers across a picture of Mason and Ike standing with Henry in front of a small white frame house. "Did Henry adopt you?"

Mason shook his head. "We were an unofficial family."

"The authorities just let you stay there? How does that happen in this day and age?"

"We lived on the reservation back then. I'm sure it would be different now, but nobody seemed very worried about me after my mother died. Frankly, I think they were just glad Henry was willing to take me."

"Why would they be glad? You were just a boy."

He shrugged, surprisingly touched by her emotional response and disconcerted by his unexpected urge to actually talk about his childhood. "You know what they say. The sins of the mother and all that."

Jolene knit her brows. "What do you mean by that?"

"It's nothing," he said, reaching for one of the library books she'd brought. "I just didn't grow up in the best of families."

"Is that why you don't like talking about your past?"

"That's part of it."

"What's the other part?"

"It's nothing," he said again, trying not to let her hear his aggravation. He'd spent too many years dodging the truth, too much time and energy making sure his childhood stayed buried. "Forget I said anything. Have you had a chance to read any of these books?"

To his surprise Jolene laughed. "Forget you said anything? Have you forgotten who you're talking to? I'm a cop, Mason. Give me an intriguing secret, and I'll be all over it."

"Even when it's something a friend doesn't want you to know about?"

The light in her eyes dimmed. "I would never betray the trust of a friend, but I am curious about why you resist talking about your childhood."

"Like I said, I didn't grow up in the best of circumstances."

Jolene smiled. "That doesn't really answer the question. Lots of people grow up in less than ideal circumstances and a whole bunch of them can't *stop* talking about what went wrong."

Mason laughed and felt himself relax. "If what you're after is a creepy story, I could give you one."

"Go ahead. I'm tough, and keeping your feelings about it bottled up probably isn't doing you any good."

Mason tried to laugh again, but it caught in his throat. When was the last time he'd talked to anyone about his childhood? He rubbed his face again and gulped iced tea, nursing a fleeting wish for something stronger. "I don't know why we're talking about this," he said, gruff-voiced. "We're here to work through your stuff."

She reached across the couch and put her hand on his arm. Her skin was warm and soft, her touch so gentle it reached him in forgotten places. "What happened when you were a kid, Mason? I'd really like to know."

"Can we just say that my mother wasn't like other mothers and leave it at that?"

"If that's what you really want."

She was waiting for him to say something, but he couldn't form the words. On impulse, or maybe out of desperation, he leaned forward and touched his mouth to hers. He wasn't expecting the burst of heat inside, or the sudden need to fold her into his arms and hold her close. He wasn't expecting her to respond, either, but she did, parting her lips and inviting his kiss. Her breath was warm and sweet, her breasts surprisingly full and soft where they crushed against his chest. She sighed, the barest whisper of sound, but it set him on fire. Only knowing that Debra was in the other room, awake, and that she could come out and find them at any time restrained him.

He ended the kiss reluctantly, far sooner than he wanted to. The flush on her cheeks and the mixture of desire and confusion in her eyes made him ache to kiss her again.

He brushed her cheek with the backs of his

fingers, then forced himself to move back to the other corner of the couch. "Have you had a chance to look through any of those books?"

Disappointment darkened her eyes, but she nodded. "One or two, but it's like reading a history textbook, and history never was my strong suit. I'm more interested in what life is like today…"

Mason gave her a strange look. "Okay, then. Be prepared to encounter prejudice."

Jolene winced, remembering that night at McGillicuddy's and a thousand such incidents before it. She still hadn't told Ryan the whole truth, and she still couldn't say why. How could she sit here with Mason, sharing dinner, laughing with his daughter, *kissing him,* and still be so worried about what Ryan and the rest of the squad would say if she told them about her heritage?

She felt horrible about it—but apparently not horrible enough. "Got it. Prejudice."

"You run into it everywhere. Grocery store. Gas station. Restaurants. Some people don't care. Some people don't notice. But there's a lot of ugliness out there, so don't be too surprised if you're victimized by it."

"Thanks for the warning. What do you know about…my family?"

"Billy's mother is still alive. He has a couple of brothers, and they have I don't know how many kids between them."

Would she ever get used to thinking of them as grandmother, uncles and cousins? She wondered what he'd think of her if he knew how uncertain she felt. When she realized that he was waiting for her to say something, she blurted the first question that came to mind. "Do you know where they are?"

"Ike does. I can introduce you when you're ready."

"Have you told anyone about me?"

Mason drained half of his tea. "You asked me not to say anything."

She added trustworthy to his list of good qualities and smiled. "Thank you. What can you tell me about the Clans I read about? There are seven?"

Mason nodded. "Right. The numbers four and seven play a big part in the Cherokee belief system. Four represents familiar forces like the cardinal directions: north, south—"

"East and west," she finished for him. "Got it." She watched his hand circle his glass and tried to forget how those fingers had felt against her cheek when he kissed her.

"There are actually seven directions," he said. "Those four, plus above, below and in the center where you are. Certain colors are associated with the four directions. Red symbolizes east, or success and triumph. Blue symbolizes north—defeat or trouble. West is symbolized by black. That's also symbolic of death. South is white, or peace and happiness."

And which one symbolized where she was at this moment? Triumphant, troubled or filled with peace and happiness? Perhaps it was possible to experience them all at the same time?

"Henry lived and breathed this stuff, and he spoon-fed it to Ike and me with every meal."

"And why did you turn away from it?" She realized the second the words left her mouth that she shouldn't have asked. She started to apologize, but he spoke before she could.

"Because it killed my mother."

Stunned silence. Jolene didn't know which of them was more surprised by his answer. A dozen responses rose to her lips, but they all sounded weak and useless.

"The number also represents the seven clans of the Cherokee," Mason went on, as if he hadn't just dropped a bombshell. "Each of the Clans is associated with a specific direction. The Wolf Clan—*Aniwayha*—is the largest. It's where most of the War Chiefs came from. They're keepers of the Wolf and traditionally the only Cherokee who can kill a wolf."

How did this kill your mother? He kept talking, but she barely registered what he was saying.

"*Anisahoni* is the Blue Clan or the Panther Clan, those who keep our children healthy. The *Anigilohi* is the Long Hair Clan or the Twister Clan or the Hair Hanging Down Clan—the Peace Chiefs. The *Anitsisqua* is the Bird Clan. Our messengers. Keepers of the birds. The *Aniwodi*, or Paint Clan, were the sorcerers and medicine men. The *Aniawi*, the Deer Clan, are keepers and hunters of the deer, and the *Anigatogeoi* or

Wild Potato Clan gathered the wild potatoes to make bread for food. That's it in a nutshell. A very small nutshell."

He met her gaze then, his own expression steady and controlled. The message clear: Don't ask.

"Mason, talk to me about her. Please."

"There's nothing to say. She died a long time ago."

"And obviously you're still hurting."

"I'm fine," he said, as she watched him draw further into himself.

"Anybody with half a brain would be able to tell that you're not fine. Your daughter is begging you to tell her about her family, and you're locked up so tightly nobody can reach you."

He stood, putting more distance between them. "Everybody has their own issues," he said, his voice cool and distant. "You have yours. I have mine."

"But at least I talk about mine."

"To me. Not to anyone who can actually make a difference. You have no right to sit in judgment of me, Jolene."

She scrambled to her feet and put herself at eye level with him again. "I'm not sitting in judgment of you," she said. "I just don't understand. Okay, so you had some bad things happen. Do you think I don't see bad things every day? Do you think anything you can tell me would shock me?"

"It's not that."

"Then what is it? You're afraid of what Debra will think? Whether you're comfortable with the past or not, Debra has a right to know the truth about her family. You *don't* have the right to withhold it from her—no matter what it is."

His eyes flashed. "I have every right. She's my daughter, and it's up to me to decide what I do or don't tell her, not you."

Had he really just said that? Knowing how she felt about the secrets her mother kept and her dad's complicity? She turned toward the door. "I think maybe I should go."

He made no move toward her, and if he spoke she didn't hear him.

CHAPTER SIXTEEN

IT WAS NEARLY MIDNIGHT when Jolene finally headed home. She'd been too agitated to sleep when she left Mason's, so she'd walked for a while.

It wasn't about *her,* she told herself over and over. It was about Debra. No matter what happened in the past, Debra deserved the truth. Mason could justify his decision to keep it from her a hundred different ways, but for Jolene, the bottom line was always the same.

Hoping she'd exhausted herself enough to sleep, she crossed the broad patch of lawn. A second-floor window glowed blue with the reflection of a television set, and a dog in the next building barked twice as she reached the sidewalk.

A soft sound caught her attention and an instant later, her father loomed large on the front steps. Three short weeks ago, looking at him she'd felt only love. The love was still there, but she couldn't get past her anger. The betrayal cut so deep she wondered if she'd ever be able to get beyond it, and she was so emotionally worn-out right now, she didn't want to find out.

"Jolene?"

She looked at him uncertainly. "Dad."

He moved out of the shadows into the dim light of the porch lamp. "I've been waiting for hours. I was afraid you wouldn't come home tonight."

"I didn't know you were here." She might not have come home if she had.

Even in the dim light, she saw him smile sadly. "Your mother and I have been trying to reach you for days. You haven't returned our calls."

She didn't know what to say to him. "I've been busy."

"We need to talk, pumpkin."

Not yet! she thought in a sudden panic. She didn't want to say things she might regret. "Can this wait? It's late, it's been a long day and I need to be up early."

"Don't you think this has waited too long already?"

"Maybe, but I'm not ready to talk about it."

That sad smile again. "If your mother and I hadn't felt that way for so long, we wouldn't be in this mess now."

He was right. "Fine," she said, her voice sharp. "You might as well come inside. It's chilly out here."

Looking almost pathetically grateful, her father followed her into the living room. She sat at one end of the couch, drawing her knees up to her chest, wrapping her arms around them, and trying not to notice all his features she once thought they shared. He settled into a chair near the window and leaned forward, elbows on his knees, staring at the floor as if it might yield some answers.

After what seemed like forever, he looked into her eyes. "It was never our intention to hurt you," he said, his voice thick with emotion. "Never. Knowing that we have is killing your mother and me."

"If you expect me to say I understand—"

He cut her off with the wave of a hand. "I know how horrible this must be for you, and I don't blame you for being angry. You deserve the truth."

Her argument with Mason had left her

emotional and vulnerable, and she knew that the best way to keep herself from boiling over was to remain very still and say nothing.

Her father ran one hand along the back of his neck and stood. "I'm going to start at the beginning." He paused, and she inclined her head once and gave him permission to go ahead.

"Your mother and I met not long after Billy was killed. She was devastated. One minute she was young and in love, and the next she was widowed and pregnant. Her parents had all but disowned her when she married Billy, and she knew she couldn't turn to them."

"And knowing that my own grandparents disapproved of me is supposed to make me feel better?" She laughed softly and shook her head. "For the record, it doesn't."

"They disapproved of Billy," he said. "They wouldn't have disapproved of you. But it was our secret, your mother's and mine. We saw no reason to tell anyone else. Your grandparents loved you, and we didn't want to create issues for you where none needed to exist."

"So you lied to them, as well. You forced

them to feel something they wouldn't have felt if they'd known I was Billy's daughter. That my genetic makeup wasn't pristine White, Anglo-Saxon Protestant."

"What your grandparents felt or didn't feel is beside the point," her father said. "I fell in love with your mother the minute I met her. I would have done anything to make her happy, and I would have died to take away her fear. I never expected her to agree to marry me. It was an insane idea, really. We were practically strangers, and I knew for a fact she didn't love me. But she wanted desperately to protect you and I provided her a way to do that. I think that's what finally won her over."

He drummed his fingers on the arm of the chair. "I hoped she might grow fond of me some day. I never dreamed she might actually fall in love with me, but I count it one of the greatest blessings of my life that she did. Having the chance to be your father is the other."

The depth of his emotion wrenched Jolene's heart, but his love for her wasn't at issue. Neither was her parents' love for each other. "Dad, I—"

"Let me finish, Jolene. Please." He perched

on the opposite arm of the couch. "From the minute you were born, I was lost. The nurse placed you in my arms, and I knew why I'd been put on this earth. I was thrilled when Trevor came along, too, but that moment I first laid eyes on you was it for me. I don't know why Billy had to die. I don't know why you weren't allowed the chance to know him. But I do know I was supposed to be your father. Nothing you or anyone else can say will ever change my mind."

Her emotion was so intense and heavy, she didn't know what to say. She imagined Mason having a talk like this with Debra someday. Secrets. What good were they? What protection did they offer, really? No matter how painful the truth might be, it would almost certainly hurt more if it was hidden.

Her father met her gaze steadily. "Should your mother and I have told you the truth? Probably. But we didn't. Not because we wanted to hurt you, but because we thought it was best."

He looked as if he wanted to touch her, but he held back. "I had my own selfish reasons for keeping the truth from you. I loved being your daddy, and I didn't want to share that honor with anyone else."

"But that wasn't your choice to make."

He shook his head and looked away. "At the time, I thought it was my choice. It's a human foible, I guess, to believe that we can make something true if we want it to be badly enough. All I'm saying is that we made some foolish decisions we probably shouldn't have made, and every time the opportunity to tell you the truth came up and we chose not to, we boxed ourselves further into the lie we'd created. But that doesn't make us bad people, honey. We're still the parents who love you and would do anything to make you happy— even if we do occasionally screw up rather badly."

"I know you love me," she whispered. "And logically, I understand and agree with everything you're saying. But this really isn't logical is it? All my life I've thought of myself as your daughter. I've pinpointed the things I thought I inherited from you and I've been proud of them. Then all of a sudden, after *thirty years,* I discover that nothing I knew about myself is true. I don't have your toes, I didn't inherit a single thing from you and I'm not related to anyone on your side of the family."

Her muscles cramped, and she kicked her feet to the floor and stood. "I know you want me to put it behind me and move on, Dad. I know it would make things much easier if I did. But I honestly don't know if I can."

"You're not the kind of person to stay angry, Jolene."

"I don't know what kind of person I am. I don't even know who I am."

"You are exactly who you've always been."

"No, I'm not! I've always been your daughter, not Mom's, and certainly not Billy Starr's. But now we both know that's not true, don't we?"

He recoiled slightly, and she regretted causing the hurt she saw in his eyes, but the past ten days had been too much for her and she couldn't seem to shut off the words. "I can't forgive you and Mom for this. Not yet, anyway. Not until I figure a few things out. I need to be able to look in the mirror and know who's looking back at me." She heard the soft ring of his cell phone, realized that her mother had been waiting for answers, and panicked.

She crossed to the door and jerked it open. "You need to go now."

"Jolene, please." He stood there for a minute as if he actually thought she might change her mind. "Just tell me if you're planning on coming to the house a week from Sunday."

The question caught her off guard, and she had to do some quick mental calculations. "That's not our usual Sunday."

"No, it's not. It's Mother's Day."

The phone rang again and Jolene's stomach tightened painfully. She'd always been the one to take charge of Mother's Day, and the fact that it had completely slipped her mind showed her just how distracted she really was. "I don't know," she said, her voice low. "I don't know if I can."

Disappointment tugged at her father's face, making him look older than Jolene had ever seen him. "At least think about it."

"Dad, please—"

"*Think* about it, Jolene."

"Fine," she said, eager to have him gone

before her mother called again. "Now please go. I need to be alone right now."

He stopped at the door and looked down at her with anguish in his eyes. "Will you call me in a few days?"

"As soon as I can."

He nodded and stepped out into the night. Jolene felt guilty about sending him away, but she ignored it. She shut the door and stood with her back pressed against it listening to her father's footsteps move away. Only then did she allow herself to cry.

CAPTAIN EISLEY PULLED Jolene into his office almost the second she walked through the door the following afternoon. That was never a good sign. Walking into the captain's office and finding your partner there before you was even worse.

Instantly wary, Jolene sat in the empty chair and waited for the storm. She didn't have to wait long.

"Ryan here's been telling me about your ideas," the captain said. His voice sounded calm enough, but the glint in his eye warned her she was on shaky ground. "Let me see if I have this straight. You've worked out this scenario in your head and you want me to okay wasting department resources on pursuing it, even though there's not one scrap of evidence to support it. Does that about wrap it up?"

Her argument with Mason had left her feeling raw all over. The visit from her father had only made things worse. The last thing Jolene needed was this. She looked at Ryan, for a sign of support, but he sat leaning forward, head bent, refusing to meet her eyes.

Well. That was that, then. At least she knew where things stood between them. "I'm asking for a couple more days, that's all," she said, struggling to keep her voice level. "I'd like to talk with Red's mother, now that we know he has one. I'd also like to spend more time with OC. I think he knows more than he's telling us."

"Even if he does, he didn't talk before. What makes you think he'll share that information with you now?"

Her stomach rolled over a couple of times, but Jolene kept her expression neutral. "I don't mean to sound flippant sir, but convincing witnesses to share what they know is part of the job. I'll find a way."

Scowling so hard his bulldog jowls quivered, Eisley waved one hand toward the bullpen. "I've got a hundred open cases sitting in our files out there. I've got a new meth lab somewhere in the city that's churning out crank faster than we can contain it, and you want to track down a missing junkie."

"Only because I'm convinced he can help us nail Zika. If we could do that—"

"Spare me the lecture, Jolene. I'm well aware what getting Raoul Zika behind bars would do. I wish you'd been more concerned about that when we had him up against the wall three weeks ago."

"I've always been concerned, Captain." Though she was no longer sure she'd ever convince him of that. "Losing Zika that night was not my fault. I did everything I could—"

Eisley cut her off. "Let's not play games. We both know what happened that night."

"With all due respect sir, I don't think we do. You're convinced I screwed up in some way, and I don't believe that's true."

Eisley shook his head, and his expression changed subtly. "I'm not blaming you, Jolene. Ultimately, the blame lies at my door.

I'm the one who sent you out there. I should have sent Santini and Ross, but I didn't."

The implication that she was inept left a bad taste in her mouth—far worse than suggesting she'd merely lost focus. "Again, I have to disagree. Santini and Ross wouldn't have been able to bring Zika in, either. That kid would have bolted no matter who was in that alley with him."

Eisley sat and his chair creaked in protest. "Let's at least face the facts here, okay? You saw a couple of kids, and that protective instinct kicked in. Nothing wrong with that. Nothing wrong with that at all. There are plenty of positions where that's exactly what's needed. Some of them are even on the police force. I just think you'll be happier if you play to your strengths than if you insist on staying here, where, frankly, the fit isn't exactly tailor-made."

"What happened that night had nothing to do with the fact that I'm a woman," she argued. "Ryan and I did all anyone could have done under the circumstances."

Eisley sat back in his chair and laced his fingers across his stomach. "The problem is, we'll never know whether that's true or not, will we? And you're asking me to let you spend department resources to chase down what I believe is a dead end. What would you do if you were in my shoes?"

"I'd leave no stone unturned, Captain. Not if it meant locking up Raoul Zika."

The captain kept his eyes locked on Jolene's as he asked, "What about you, Fielding? What do you think? Worth pursuing or wild-goose chase?"

Ryan shifted uncomfortably in his chair and Jolene held her breath. After an unconscionably long time, he inclined his head. "It might be worth pursuing, Captain. At least for a couple more days."

Eisley narrowed his eyes and shifted away from Jolene to Ryan. "You believe this cockamamy story?"

"Let's just say I don't *not* believe it."

Not a ringing endorsement, but she could hardly expect more from a partner who'd go behind her back in the first place.

Color crept into Captain Eisley's cheeks and he wagged his head in disbelief. "All right, then. Go. But I'm not wasting forty-eight hours on this. I'll give you until the end of your shift today. Unless you come up with

something concrete to prove Red's alive and
that he knows something solid about Zika,
don't ask me for one second longer. You got
that?"

Jolene got to her feet. "Got it, Captain.
And thank you."

"Just do your job, Preston. Show me that
you can hold your own around here."

Oh, she would. Somehow. Though just
how she'd do it was a mystery.

CHAPTER SEVENTEEN

JOLENE WAITED TO CONFRONT Ryan until they were in the car, driving across town to the address of Vivienne Beck's parents. This wasn't a conversation she wanted to have at the station where Santini and Ross, or anyone else on the squad, could hear them.

This was between her and her partner.

She thought surely Ryan could tell how angry she was, but he seemed oblivious. "You're quiet this afternoon. Any special reason?"

Was he serious? "I'm just trying to figure out what happened back there. Why were you and Eisley so chummy before I got there?"

Ryan shrugged. "I got there before you. He wanted to know where we were on the case. I told him what you told me. No big deal."

That sounded plausible, even if it didn't explain why he'd been unable to meet her gaze while they were there. She thought about asking him to explain that, but she couldn't go there. She knew how Eisley felt about having a woman on the squad. She knew how guys like Santini and Ross felt. But raise the issue of gender bias aloud? Not if she hoped to ever earn the respect of her colleagues. Crying foul was the quickest way she knew of to get herself ostracized. She'd seen it happen before.

She forced a smile and watched houses, stores and businesses pass in a blur. "Thanks for agreeing with me back there. I owe you one."

"Yeah? Well I just hope you're right. We could use some good news." He was silent for a few blocks, then asked, "What's happening on the home front, Jo? Have you talked to your parents yet?"

They'd avoided talking about this for so long, she wasn't ready with an answer. She didn't want to create any more tension between them, so she skirted the truth. "Yeah. My dad stopped by for a little while last night, as a matter of fact."

"You guys have worked everything out then?"

She thought about just saying yes, but he'd figure out the truth eventually, so she took the middle ground. "We're working on it. That's really all you can say after a thing like this."

Ryan took his eyes off the road for a second. "You met any of your new family yet?"

Her second lie hit a little further from the truth. "Not yet, but soon."

"Well, that's good." Apparently satisfied, Ryan switched topics again. "It's weird to think of someone like Red having a family, isn't it?"

Jolene gradually let herself relax. "You can say that again."

"You really think his mother knows where to find him?"

"I think it's possible. You heard what Vivienne said yesterday. The mom's a real pushover when it comes to Red, and since he walked away with two thousand dollars the last time they saw each other, I'd say Vivienne is probably right. If Red is planning to hide out for a while, he's going to need more than two grand. My guess is he's counting on Mom to supply it."

"That's probably a safe bet," Ryan agreed. "So the next question is, will she tell us what she knows?"

"Not if she thinks we're a danger to him."

"Us?" Ryan slowed, checked street signs, and turned into a subdivision that had probably been build in the early sixties. Some of the houses were still well kept, but others were starting to show signs of neglect. "What kind of danger could a couple of nice guys like us pose to good old Red?"

Jolene grinned as he turned into a cul-de-sac. "Let's hope we can convince Mommy Dearest to see it the same way."

The Beck home was a two-story job nestled in the trees at the top of the circle. If it was hard to imagine Big Red having parents and a sister, it was even harder to imagine him growing up in a nice, normal neighborhood like this one.

Jolene walked with Ryan up the curved sidewalk to the front door and remembered what Mason had said about watching Debra self-destruct and feeling powerless to stop her. Did Red's parents feel the same way?

Ryan pressed the doorbell and a slim woman with short auburn hair answered. If she bore any resemblance to Red besides the hair color, Jolene couldn't see it. While Red was well over six feet and husky, Naomi Beck was short, slim and almost fragile looking.

Just as Vivienne had, she recognized who they were before they could open their mouths. Resignation and deep sadness washed across her features. "You're here about Russell, aren't you?"

Jolene nodded. "Yes, ma'am. I'm Sergeant Preston, and this is Detective Fielding with the Tulsa Police Department."

"Is he all right? You're not here to tell me he's dead, are you?"

"No, ma'am. We're trying to locate him. Have you seen Russell or heard from him recently?"

"Not since the middle of April." She stepped away from the door and motioned them inside. "You might as well come in. I'm sure you have other questions. You people always do."

She led them into a modest living room dominated by a piano covered with framed photographs. Jolene gave the photos a cursory glance and felt a tug of emotion when she looked at one of Red as a teenager, bright and eager, one arm draped casually around his sister's skinny shoulders. In another, he was beaming as he held up a string of fish from some weekend outing with his father.

There was nothing visible that made her life different from Red's, so how could two people from loving homes wind up on such different paths? Had her parents been more involved in her life? More watchful? Less harsh? Had the boundaries been more visible? Or less? Had Red come upon a crossroads one day, similar to the one Debra was facing now? Had his parents taken a wrong turn then? What had they done differently with Vivienne to turn her into a productive member of society?

"My daughter told me that the police had been by to see her at work. Was it you two?"

Ryan nodded. "Yesterday."

"So you want to know about the money Russell took from me."

"Yes ma'am," he said. "And we need to know if you've heard from him or seen him since he took the money."

"He's in trouble, isn't he?"

"Not with us," Jolene assured her. "Did he say anything to you about being in some kind of trouble?"

Naomi waved one small, birdlike hand in front of her. "No. But he's been in trouble since he was fifteen. Living out there the way he does, around those people... Every time there's a knock on the door or the phone rings, I'm afraid one of you is going to tell me he's gone."

That might be soon if Jolene's instincts were correct. "He may be in trouble, Mrs. Beck. We think he may have stumbled across some information he shouldn't have, and now he's hiding to protect himself. If that's true—if he has information about the people we think he does—then we need to find him. We can't help him if we don't know where he is."

Naomi's pale eyes widened. "What kind of information?"

"We don't know," Jolene said. "So far it's a lot of speculation and gut instinct. All I can tell you is that he's not in any danger from the police."

Ryan spoke, his voice low and gentle.

"Can you tell us where to find him, Mrs. Beck?"

Naomi shook her head. "I'm sorry. I don't know where he is."

"When you saw him in April," Jolene said, "did he say anything unusual? Mention any names?"

"No, but I only saw him for a minute."

"He didn't mention plans to meet somebody? Talk about an appointment? Anything?"

Naomi shook her head slowly. "I'm sorry," she repeated. "He doesn't talk to me about the people he knows."

Disappointed, Jolene wasn't ready to give up yet. "Do you think he might have said something to his father?"

"Spencer hasn't spoken to Russell in years."

"But he knows you've remained in touch with him," Jolene said. "He knows about the money Russell took?"

Naomi stiffened. "Borrowed."

Jolene met Ryan's gaze and saw her own skepticism mirrored in his eyes. "Of course," Ryan said, his voice carefully neutral. "Your husband knows about the money?"

"Yes, he knows." Naomi's hands fluttered in front of her. "My husband has a hard time dealing with Russell. Spencer just doesn't understand Russell the way I do."

"And how's that?"

"Russell was always a quiet, sensitive boy. Things hit him hard. He doesn't cope well. I'm sure that's why he started using drugs the way he did."

Eager for any insight into Red's thought processes, Jolene asked, "When was that? How old was he?"

"Fourteen. It was after his grandmother died. He was a model student and a perfect son until then. Straight *A*s. Student Council."

Jolene tried to readjust her image of the burly, bearded Red with the portrait his mother painted. It wasn't easy.

"When he started having trouble," Naomi went on, "Spencer just couldn't deal with it. It caused a lot of friction in the family. I'm sure that's why Russell eventually left home."

She certainly had a rich fantasy life, Jolene mused. "What did your husband do to drive him away?"

"He wanted to send Russell to a boot camp. Where they treat the kids like…like—"

"Like criminals?" Ryan suggested.

The look Naomi gave him could have frozen fire. "I realize that those places work on some people, but it would have been the wrong thing for Russell."

"You were able to keep him from going?" Jolene guessed.

"I had to. For Russell's sake."

"And you started meeting Russell away from here?"

"I *had* to," she said again. "Spencer doesn't want him to come around here."

"Did you meet him somewhere else in April?" Ryan asked.

"Yes."

"Russell called you?"

"He sent me a message, yes."

"Why did he want to see you?"

Naomi's expression grew stern. "He's my son. What reason does he need?"

"According to Vivienne, he left with two thousand dollars," Ryan pointed out. "How did that happen?"

"I gave it to him. I know he doesn't have much. I know how he struggles. He tries and tries, but he can't hold down a job, and he barely scrapes by. He's too proud to ask, but I know when he needs money."

"So you gave him your ATM card?"

"He didn't want to take it. He tried to tell me he'd be fine. He had some deal cooking—that's the way he put it. A deal cooking. He said he was going to be bringing in money from that."

Jolene's heart slowed ominously and she looked at Ryan. "What kind of deal?"

"He didn't tell me. He wouldn't. Like I said, he never talks about his life out there."

"But he was expecting money?"

"He said he'd be set for life if he could just pull everything together."

Set for life. *Blackmail.* He was going to get himself killed if he hadn't already. "Where do you go to meet Russell?"

"I can't tell you that. Russell trusts me."

The woman was rapidly fraying Jolene's patience, but Jolene tried to keep her voice clear and calm. "Mrs. Beck, Russell may be in danger. We want to help him, but we can't do that if you won't help us. Where can we find Russell?"

"I don't know." Naomi said, but for the

first time, she seemed agitated. "I don't know where he is now, but there's a place in Riverside Park where we meet."

"Where? What place?"

"The fountain. The one with the bears."

"The new one on the Plaza?"

"Yes. You know where it is?"

Jolene nodded. "How do you know when to meet him? Does he call you?"

Naomi shook her head again. "No. He wouldn't dare. His father might answer."

"Then how?"

"He sends me a note. Sometimes he'll get word to me through his sister."

That didn't help at all. Maybe it was knowing that Red had once been twelve, that he had a name and a family—that his mother thought of him as sensitive and his sister still cared about him made the need to find him even more urgent. "If you wanted to get word to him, if you wanted to ask him to meet you there, how would you do it? Please, Mrs. Beck."

Naomi stared, surprised, at Jolene. "But I can't. I don't have any way of contacting him. I only see Russell when he comes to me."

IT WAS ALMOST DARK by the time Jolene and Ryan pulled up in front of the GemCrest Toys warehouse. They'd spent the past couple of hours tracking down people who knew Red and trying to find someone— anyone—who knew where to find him.

Ryan parked beneath a streetlight and they sat for a minute, sizing up the activity in the parking lot. The warehouse was disturbing enough in the daylight. By night even the most hardened officers took extra precautions when they had to come here.

Unlike the last time Jolene and Ryan were here, people stood in clusters around the parking lot, watching Jolene and Ryan with suspicion. Like vampires, this segment of society came to life when the sun went down, and they trusted no one—especially not one another.

"What do you think our chances are of finding OC here at this time of night?" she asked Ryan.

Ryan unbuckled his seat belt and reached for the door latch. "How lucky are you feeling?"

That was the trouble. She wasn't feeling lucky at all. With only a few hours until the end of their shift, defeat loomed in front of her. She didn't think Naomi Beck's claim that Red had some kind of deal in the works would be enough to convince Captain Eisley, and they still hadn't found an iota of evidence. But she couldn't return to the station empty-handed. She knew in her heart that Red's life depended on what they found tonight, and so did her career.

"Let's check around out here first," Ryan suggested. "Maybe somebody knows where OC is."

Jolene nodded and stepped out into the gathering darkness. She'd never been one to admit defeat easily; she'd never backed away from a fight. But tonight she could almost feel another life change in the offing.

She and Ryan worked together, moving around the parking lot from group to group, asking if anyone had seen Big Red or knew where to find OC, getting nowhere with the answers. Her mood dropped lower with each conversation, and she entertained thoughts of going back to the station and admitting defeat.

She was just about to suggest it to Ryan when she spotted a shadowy figure near the corner of the warehouse. He was a large crate of a man, wearing an oversize sweatshirt with the hood pulled low over his eyes, and dirty cargo pants at least two sizes too big. Everything about him, from his size to the way he moved, put her senses on alert.

She couldn't see him well enough to know if it was Red or just someone who looked a whole lot like him, but she wasn't about to let him get away until she found out. With her heart in her throat, she told herself to be cool. Don't let him sense that she'd noticed him. But waiting for Ryan to finish talking with Misty, a working girl so hopped up on cocaine she barely knew her own name, was almost more than she could stand.

When he finally moved away, Jolene fell into step beside him, close enough to rub shoulders. Hopefully close enough to keep her voice from carrying.

"I think he's here," she said.

"Who?"

"Red. I think that's him over by the corner."

She moved away from Ryan, putting enough distance between them to let him glance around without being obvious. His gaze swept the parking lot, passed over the shadowy figure without pause, and he dipped his head almost imperceptibly. But Red must have been watching closely because that slight dip of the head was enough to spur him to action.

With surprising agility, he sprinted the short distance to the steps, bolted up them two at a time and disappeared inside the warehouse.

Ryan was on the move before Red even reached the bottom of the steps. "You take the outside," he shouted over his shoulder. "I'm going in."

Instinct kicked in, and with it a rush of adrenaline. Jolene drew her Beretta and raced along the length of the building, leaping over piles of rotting garbage, dodging clusters of empty beer cans, crunching through broken glass.

She'd skipped her run for the past few days, and she could feel it in her legs and lungs, but she ignored the discomfort and kept going. She'd lost one chance at Zika, she wasn't going to lose another.

At the far end of the building, she stopped running. Every cell in her body screamed at her to hurry before Red got away, but she couldn't afford to take chances. Keeping her back to the wall, she peered around the corner and tried to take stock of her surroundings. It was too dark to see much, but there didn't seem to be much to see. She could make out the hulking shapes of two Dumpster containers in the distance, an abandoned loading dock and two sets of metal stairs flanking it, each one leading to a door to the inside.

She inched forward, watching for any sign of movement, straining to hear any sound besides her own breathing. Another five feet and she'd be caught in the glow of the moonlight, exposed and unprotected. She stayed close to the building, as deep in the shadows as she could, hoping they would hide her as effectively as they seemed to hide everything else.

Silence permeated the area, and her heartbeat seemed loud enough to set off car alarms. She climbed the first set of steps and tried the door, just in case. The knob must have been rusted because it didn't even move beneath her fingers.

Between one breath and the next, the hair

on her neck stood up and she realized that someone or something was behind her. She whipped around, Beretta raised, but she was too late. Someone roughly the size of a refrigerator slammed into her and sent her tumbling over the metal railing. She hit her head against it on her way down, and she felt the burn of pain as something sharp tore her thigh. The last thing she was aware of before everything went black was the sickening crunch of bone as she struck the pavement.

CHAPTER EIGHTEEN

JUST AFTER NOON four days later, Jolene shut off the engine of the 4Runner in the long, narrow parking lot in front of the Cherokee Cultural Center and rested the cast on her left arm on the steering wheel. Her head throbbed. The bandage on her right leg pulled tight around the swelling, and the gash she'd sustained when she hit the concrete stairs pounded with every heartbeat, but by far the worst of her injuries was to her pride.

She'd been lying around her apartment since Ryan brought her home from the emergency room, staring at her four walls, thinking way too much about Mason and Debra, wishing she had the nerve to call him. She hoped that Ryan and his temporary partner would be able to track Big Red down again. At least Captain Eisley finally believed Red was in hiding. That was something.

She'd overdosed on daytime television the very first day, she'd pored over the library books Mason had suggested for her and she'd even read a couple of good mysteries, but it all seemed like so much busywork. She ached to *do* something, but Captain Eisley wouldn't let her come back to work for at least a week. Even that wasn't guaranteed.

Maybe it was a good thing. She'd been avoiding coming here for nearly a month already. Time to stop running away.

She climbed out of the car and stood on the sidewalk looking at the long, low building, trying to absorb the fact that she belonged here. Just over there, her birth parents had posed for the cameras. Her mother had been younger than Jolene was now and, by all accounts, starry-eyed in love. With a stranger.

That stranger—Billy—should have been the man who'd come to talk to her on Friday night. He should have been the one to talk about the day she was born, about the joys of being her father, and about the frustrations.

For the first time, she felt sad for Billy. She also felt strangely irritated that he'd earned her mother's love first.

She'd driven past this place at least a hundred times over the years, but she'd never paid much attention to it until now. How odd to think that the man who'd been responsible for building it was also responsible for her.

Everything hurt as she hitched the strap of her purse over her shoulder. She wished that she'd asked someone to come with her— but who? Her mother? Never in a million years. Not Trevor, either. No, there was only one person she wanted here.

The Center had been built with two V-shaped wings stretching away from an octagon centerpiece, where she found an information booth staffed by two women.

Museum cases stretched down one corridor, a well-stocked gift shop took up another. The third corridor held what appeared to be meeting rooms, and she could see tables, chairs and vending machines at the far end of the fourth.

The older of the two women looked up with an expectant smile when she heard the door shut. She was probably a few years over sixty, an inch or two shorter than Jolene's five-five. Her gray hair was bound in a thick braid that fell almost to her waist. *"Osiyo,"* she said. "Welcome. Can we help you find something?"

Uncharacteristically shy, Jolene shook her head. "I'd just like to look around—if that's okay?"

"Of course. Take as long as you want." The woman's brow puckered when she realized Jolene was limping and her gaze landed on Jolene's cast. "Are you all right? Can I get you something to make you more comfortable?"

"I'm fine," Jolene assured her. "Just moving a little slower than usual."

The woman didn't look convinced. "Well, if you need anything let us know. Is this your first visit to the Center?"

"Yes, it is."

"New to Tulsa, or just visiting?"

"Neither," Jolene admitted, embarrassed. "I've lived here all my life. I've just never taken the time before."

"Well, that's all right. We're always happy when neighbors come by. Is there anything special you'd like to see?"

"Nothing special. I'm interested in everything."

"Wonderful. You chose a good time to come. We're celebrating our anniversary this year, so we have several exhibits going on right now, and they're all open to the public." The woman let herself out from behind the counter and gestured toward one of the corridors. "We have a large display of paintings, baskets and jewelry made by local artisans, but you might want to look at the museum first. The history might help you understand the art."

"Actually, a friend suggested several research books so I've read quite a bit in the past few days. Maybe I'll start with the art exhibits. Where can I find them?"

"I'm going there myself, so I'll be glad to show you. I'm Thea High Eagle, by the way," the woman said, offering her hand.

The woman's grip was firm. Jolene introduced herself and fell into step beside Thea who adjusted her own pace to match Jolene's limp.

"You're going to a lot of trouble for someone with only a passing curiosity. Are you a reporter?"

"I recently found out that I'm part Cherokee. I'm just trying to find out what that means."

Thea's smile inched up a little further. "I'd say that depends on what you want it to mean."

"That's the part I don't know," Jolene admitted.

"Luckily, you have a lifetime to figure it out. If you can prove your lineage, the first thing I'd suggest would be to join the Cherokee Nation, but you can only do that if you can prove your ancestry through an entry on the Dawes Roll."

"That's the list compiled by the government to keep track of the people who were moved here during the eighteen hundreds, isn't it?"

Thea nodded. "The ones who were granted property ownership and who lived here between 1866 and 1900. So many of The People drifted off and blended into the white population to avoid being driven off their land, it's impossible to trace ancestry without the Roll."

"I think I can prove a link," Jolene said. "But I'm not ready to take a step quite that big." Worried that Thea might have been offended by that, she added, "It's just that I'm still trying to work through all of this and I don't really feel a connection yet."

Thea's smile banished her fears immediately. "I understand completely." She took Jolene's uninjured arm and led her through a set of doors into a large room that had been divided into aisles by rows of temporary dividers. Displays of baskets and beadwork lined one long wall; oil paintings, watercolors, pencil sketches and photographs had been hung throughout the rest of the display. Only a handful of people were milling about, and nobody seemed even slightly interested in Jolene's arrival. Just the way she wanted it.

"Here you are," Thea said. "You can take all the time need, so don't rush. It will come to you. What would you like to see first?"

"You don't have to stay with me," Jolene said. "I'm sure you have other things you should be doing."

"Not for a few minutes. I was just killing time when you came in. Why don't you let me show you some of my favorite pieces before I have to leave?"

Jolene wanted to experience this alone, but she couldn't think of a graceful way to refuse, so she followed Thea and soon lost herself in the artwork. Some of the paintings seemed almost primitive while others were complex and detailed, but the connection of each artist to the earth and to the past was easy to see.

They reached the end of the first aisle and had just started up the second when Thea paused in front of a large frame. Her expression changed dramatically. She stared at the painting with such intimacy and sadness, Jolene felt like an intruder.

Curious to see what had affected Thea so deeply, Jolene moved closer. The canvas was painted in bold colors, portraying a cluster of people looking on as a small group of boys danced around a fire. In the foreground, a lone pine tree stood sentinel, its branches heavy with needles. What made the painting remarkable was the onlookers' faces, twisted in anguish.

Their grief was so vivid, Jolene sucked in a quiet breath. "It's very realistic, isn't it?"

Thea nodded. "This is my favorite piece in the exhibit."

"It's magnificent. But the pain on their faces is…well, it's almost like you can feel it."

"They are mothers who are losing their sons. It's a depiction of an old Cherokee story, *Anitsutsa*, the legend of the boys. Have you heard it?"

"No. I haven't come across that one yet."

"It's a story my father used to tell me when I was a child. Of course, I shared it with my children when they were young, and now my grandchildren tell it to their children. So much of our past has been lost already."

"You have this place to keep it alive," Jolene said, surprised to discover she felt proud knowing Billy was partly responsible for that.

"It's a blessing, that's for sure."

Jolene moved closer to the painting. "Was this done by a local artist?"

"It was painted by my granddaughter."

"Really? Then you must be very proud."

"I'm proud of all my grandchildren. I'm a very lucky woman." Thea pointed toward the circle of dancers on the canvas. "The legend says that when the world was new, there were seven boys who spent all their time down by the townhouse playing the *gatayû'stï* game. The boys would roll a stone wheel along the ground and try to hit it with a curved stick. Their mothers scolded the boys for playing instead of working, but boys then were the same as boys now, I guess. They ignored their mothers until one day the women collected some *gatayû'stï* stones and boiled them with corn. When the boys came in, their mothers served the stones and told them that since they liked the *gatayû'stï* better than working, they could have the stones for dinner."

Jolene could just imagine Trevor's reaction to a supper of stones, and the image brought a smile to her lips. "I guess mothers are the same everywhere, too, aren't they?"

Thea laughed softly. "Some things never change. The boys were very angry, and they decided that if their mothers were going to treat them that way, they would go where they wouldn't trouble their mothers again. They began to dance round the townhouse, praying to the spirits. When the mothers went to look for the boys, they were still dancing, their feet off the ground. With every circle they made around the townhouse, they rose higher in the air. Of course, the mothers tried to get their children back, but it was too late. The boys were already above the roof of the townhouse."

She turned away from the picture. "All but one boy, whose mother managed to pull him down with the *gatayû'stï* pole. He hit the ground with such force that he sank into it and the earth closed over him. The other six boys kept circling, higher and higher, until they went up to the sky. Most people know them as the Pleiades constellation, but the Cherokee call them *Ani'tsutsä*."

Seven dancing boys, caught up and carried away, leaving their parents to grieve. She thought about Naomi Beck's concern for her son, about Mason's fear when he thought Debra was using drugs, about her parents' sadness. Jolene didn't know what the Cherokee meaning behind the legend was, but for her it would always represent the struggle between parent and child.

"What about the parents?" she asked.

"They grieved for a long time. The mother whose boy went into the ground came to cry over the spot every morning and evening until the earth was damp with her tears. After a while, a green shoot sprouted up and grew every day until it became the tall tree that we now call the pine."

Jolene slanted a glance at the older woman. "And that was the bedtime story you told your children? Did they actually sleep afterward?"

Thea laughed and stepped away from the painting. "It's the story I told my boys when they chose to disobey me. There are worse things than losing a little sleep, I'm afraid."

Jolene opened her mouth to say something else, but when she saw a tall man with dark hair and broad shoulders walk past the far end of the aisle, she forgot what she'd been about to say.

"Jolene? Are you all right?"

With an embarrassed laugh, she looked away from the now-empty spot. "Yes, I—I thought I saw someone I knew, but I'm sure I was mistaken."

"Here? Would you like to go find out?"

She shook her head quickly. Even if she was right, she hadn't seen Mason since the night of their argument. She wouldn't know what to say to him.

She struggled to pay attention to what

Thea was telling her about a large painting of a woman with an eagle, but the words faded in and out and she couldn't have repeated Thea's story if her life depended on it. Maybe Captain Eisley was right. Maybe she *wasn't* focused enough to do the job. The cast on her arm and the gash on her leg certainly seemed to prove his point.

Suddenly the man she'd spotted earlier was standing right in front of them. Even before Jolene could process that it really was Mason—with Debra, Thea gasped. "Mason Blackfox? Is that you?"

He made no effort to hide his surprise at seeing Jolene there, but he managed a smile for the older woman. "Hello, Thea. It's been a while."

"Too long." Thea's delight at seeing Mason seemed so genuine, Jolene wondered again that he could distance himself from the people he'd known as a child. "And you must be Debra," Thea said to the girl whose huge brown eyes reflected a curiosity at least equal to Jolene's. "Ike told me you were here visiting your dad. Are you having a good time so far?"

Debra curled a lip. "It's all right, I guess."

She turned her attention to Jolene. "You're all banged up. What happened?"

"I had an accident at work," Jolene said, embarrassed. "We're neighbors," she explained to Thea. "Mason's the one who suggested the books I've been reading."

"Is that right?" Thea's smile grew even warmer. "I am glad to hear that, Mason. I was afraid you'd forgotten all about us."

"I haven't forgotten," he said in that tight, clipped voice Jolene had come to recognize.

Thea didn't seem to notice. "I'm glad. It's good to remember where you come from."

"I'm just here with Debra," Mason said. "She's writing a report for school, and I promised to bring her." What he didn't say echoed in the room. *I won't be back.* And the way he so carefully avoided eye contact with Jolene made her suspect that he hadn't changed his mind about anything else, either.

Thea slipped an arm around Debra's shoulders and walked slowly, leaving Jolene and Mason to bring up the rear. "I'm sure you're curious about your people. Anything you want to know, Debra, feel free to ask. If I don't know the answers, I know where to find them."

It was an opening Jolene wouldn't have been able to pass up, and she was pretty sure Debra would take it, too. Sure enough, Debra turned that oh-so-innocent smile of hers on Thea. "There is one thing I want to know," she said, using her big brown eyes to their best advantage. "Did you know my grandparents?"

CHAPTER NINETEEN

HAD IT BEEN ANYONE but Thea High Eagle who'd just offered to tell Debra about her grandparents, Mason might've knocked some sense into them. Unfortunately, because he'd known Thea forever and he'd always respected her, because he knew how deeply showing disrespect to her would have disappointed Henry, and because Jolene was watching him like a hawk, he bit back what he really wanted to say.

But that didn't mean he had to stand idly by and let Thea expose Debra to everything he'd worked so hard to protect her from.

"I knew both of your grandparents," Thea was saying to Debra. "What do you want to know?"

"Nothing." Mason wedged himself between them and locked eyes with his daughter. "You know how I feel about that, Debra."

"Yeah. It's all some big, dark secret." Debra hooked her thumbs in her back pockets and looked at Thea. "He won't even talk to me about them."

"No, I won't, and neither will anybody else. I know you mean well, Thea, but this subject is closed."

Tiny lines formed over the bridge of Thea's nose. "Maybe you and I should talk about this."

"There's nothing to say."

"Oh, but I think there is."

The years peeled away, and he followed her toward the door feeling just as he had at eleven when Thea caught him starting the fire in the Dumpster. She'd never told Henry about that, or about half a dozen other escapades she knew about. Like it or not, he owed her more than respect.

In the corridor, she moved a safe distance from the doorway, then turned to face him. "Is there a problem?"

"Yeah, there is. I don't want Debra to know about my parents."

"Why not?"

"She's young. She's struggling with a few issues herself. I remember what it did to me when I figured out what was going on at my house, and I don't want her to go through that."

Thea's smile evaporated. "You don't think she has a right to know?"

"No, I don't."

"They were her grandparents."

"They didn't deserve to be."

"That's unworthy of you, Mason. Your mother had a rough life. There were things that happened in her childhood that affected her until the day she died. Your refusal to forgive her doesn't serve anyone."

Mason clenched his teeth so hard his jaw hurt. "That's just an excuse. We all have issues. They can stop you in your tracks if you let them. But there comes a point when a person has to take responsibility for what they do. Forget what somebody else did to them and just step up."

"Forget," Thea mused. "The way you have?"

"I'm trying, okay? And excusing my mother's choices because she had a rough childhood is just wrong."

"I'm not talking about excusing," Thea told him. "I'm talking about understanding and forgiving. You need to do that—for yourself, not for her."

How many times had Henry told him the same thing? *Forgive her, Mason. Let it go.*

"What possible good would it do to tell Debra about my parents?" he asked, hoping that if Thea stopped to think for a minute, she'd acknowledge that some things were better left alone.

"There's no way for us to know that, is there? If she's this curious, there must be a reason."

"Yeah, to make me miserable."

Thea put a hand on his arm, the way she had when his mother fell into a display of her baskets, crushing them in front of the whole community. In the murmur of voices coming from the exhibit hall, he imagined the laughter that had driven him almost crazy with embarrassment and hatred.

"I know how you feel," Thea said, pulling him back to the present with her soft voice. "I understand it. But you came to your parents for a reason. Whether you acknowledge it or not, they had something valuable to teach you. That value doesn't diminish simply because you don't approve of their methods."

"The only thing either of them ever taught me," he said, biting off each word carefully, "was the value of staying sober."

"And you discount the value of that?"

Thea's knowing smile nudged his irritation a few degrees higher. "No, but I think I could have learned it some other way."

"I'm sure you could have, but maybe it was the pain of the experience that made the lesson so memorable."

"With all due respect, Thea, I'd rather skip the philosophy lesson. All I'm asking is that you respect my wishes when it comes to Debra. Will you do that?"

He saw disapproval in her eyes, but she nodded. "If you feel that strongly about it."

She really had no idea.

PLEASANTLY FULL from the dinner she'd had delivered, Jolene carried the nearly empty Chinese food containers into the kitchen and put them in the refrigerator. She'd been trying all evening to stop thinking about Mason—and Debra, of course—but no matter what she did, they were always there.

They'd parted company after that brief conversation with Thea, and Jolene wasn't sure yet whether she was glad of that or not. Less than thirty minutes later, she'd seen Mason and Debra leaving, and she'd been dying of curiosity ever since to know how things were at their apartment.

She wondered what Mason, who seemed almost obsessed with home cooking and balanced meals, would think if he saw the pathetic contents of her fridge. Two lonely yogurt containers, a six-pack of beer, half a jar of mayonnaise and now a little shrimp lo mein and rice.

He seemed like a great guy. Hardworking. Reliable. Responsible. Honest—except, of course, when it came to his past. He seemed to genuinely love his daughter. So what was the big secret?

She closed the refrigerator door and carried the fork, spoon and chopsticks she'd used to the sink. She could see her reflection in the window, hair sticking up every which way, eyes shadowed, face pale. She noticed a dark stain on the faded white of her favorite old T-shirt, and looked down to check.

Soy sauce. All she wanted was one meal without dropping food on herself. Was that too much to ask? She wet a cloth and tried to scrub the stain out.

She only succeeded in spreading the stain around a bit and gave up, swallowed a pain pill for the throbbing in her arm and put the prescription bottle away.

Her cupboard was nearly empty. A jar of chunky peanut butter, half a loaf of bread, coffee and two cans of chicken noodle soup. Other than the bag of fun-size Snickers bars in her sock drawer, that was about it.

She made a note to hit the grocery store sometime soon, and limped back to the living room. By the time she collapsed on the couch, she'd given up the pretense. Why spend time and money at the grocery store when it would be a waste?

Other working women could go to the office at eight and come home at five, kick off their shoes, toss in a load of laundry and whip up a casserole. It wasn't so easy when your eight-to-five life was filled with drug addicts and hellholes like the GemCrest warehouse. Balance, her mother always said. Jolene fumbled for the remote.

She flipped through all the channels twice, then settled on a rerun of *Monk,* but she'd only watched about five minutes when her doorbell rang. Surprised, she turned off the TV and checked the peephole. Mason. Her heart beat faster, as she whipped open the door.

Mason's gaze traveled over her flannel Tweety Bird pajamas to her face, then circled back and started over—this time more slowly.

While Jolene appreciated his interest, she refused to stand there while he ogled her dirty shirt. "Mason? Is everything okay?"

She actually thought his cheeks flushed. "Fine. Did I come at a bad time?"

She turned a rueful glance on the soy sauce stain and flicked at a stray hair with her finger. "Is that a serious question?"

He smiled, slow and sexy. "You look good to me."

"You need your eyes checked." He was back to his regular self, and Jolene was glad to see it. "Where's Debra?"

"At home. I'd like to talk to you alone, but I can't stay long."

"That sounds serious." She stepped aside to let him come in. "I just took a pain pill so I should be coherent for about ten minutes. Think that's enough?"

"I'll talk fast."

"Perfect." She led him into the living room and sat on the couch. "I'd offer you something to drink, but you wouldn't like anything in my fridge. There's water, though. I could—"

He waved off the offer and sat beside her. "I'm fine. Don't worry about it. How was your visit to the Cultural Center?"

"Informative. Yours?"

"Not as bad as I was afraid it would be. You met Thea."

Jolene nodded. "She seems very nice."

"She is. I've known her since I was a kid. She's a tribal Elder and a master craftsman in basketry. She's been a member of the board of directors for the Cherokee National Historical Society for years, and one of her sons used to be Deputy Chief."

"Are you talking about Elwood?"

Mason shook his head. "That was Sam. Elwood is on the Environmental Protection Committee."

"Is that why you came to talk to me? Because of Thea?"

Mason nodded.

"I didn't come to tell you who she is in the tribe. I came to tell you who she is to you. I thought you ought to know."

"To *me?*"

"She's your grandmother, Jolene."

The warm glow Jolene had been feeling evaporated. "You knew who she was, and you waited until now to tell me?"

"You said you weren't ready to know about your family, and I didn't think you wanted me to make that kind of announcement in front of her."

"You're right." She pulled one of the decorative pillows onto her lap and plucked at the button in its center. She took a couple of minutes to process what he'd told her. "Did you tell her about me?"

Mason shook his head. "I promised I wouldn't, but I think you should tell her."

"Me?"

"You want me to? I can."

She shook her head quickly. "Tempting… but no."

"She's an incredible woman, and she's very big on family. I think you'll like her when you get to know her."

"She's different from what I expected."

"What did you expect?"

"I don't know. She was…" Every word that came to mind sounded wrong. Insulting. What *had* she expected? An old native woman with skin wrinkled by the sun? Someone who barely spoke English? She was as bad as her maternal grandparents. "She was younger than I expected," she said, grasping at the only thing she could think of.

"She's probably in her midseventies by now. It's good you're coming into her life while there's time."

Jolene ran back over their conversation, suddenly greedy to remember every detail. "That means that the artist who painted those floating boys is my cousin?"

"One of about a dozen. Most of them are married with kids of their own."

"Are they all involved with the Center?"

"Not all of them."

"Do they all live around here?"

"Most of them. The whole family is very close."

Instinctively, Jolene tried to pull her knees up against her chest, but moving her thigh that much sent burning pain through her leg. She gasped. "Bad idea," she murmured, closing her eyes while she struggled to get the pain under control.

She opened them again to find Mason watching her from beneath beetle brows. "Are you all right?"

She tried to joke, but her voice came out high and tight. "Compared to what?"

He didn't laugh. In fact, he looked annoyed. "Are you going to tell me what happened, or just leave me quietly going crazy with curiosity and worry?"

It was probably wrong to let the concern on his face make her feel so good inside, but she couldn't help herself. "It was an accident at work.".

"So you told Debra. What kind of accident?"

"I fell."

"From where? The top of a building?"

"No, just down a flight of stairs."

"How?"

She could have told him a dozen stories to make the incident sound less threatening, less dangerous, but she had the disconcerting feeling that he'd be able to see right through them all. "My partner and I have been looking for someone. I got caught off guard."

The concern on his face grew with every word. "Somebody did this to you?"

"Being injured is a risk that comes with the job."

"And your families know it."

"It comes with the territory, Mason. All things considered, the risk is relatively minor." She was used to seeing the worry in her parents' eyes, but the look on Mason's face was new and it hit her hard. She couldn't afford to have that image in her head when she went back to work or she'd freeze up for sure.

"You have a broken arm," he said with a jerk of his chin toward her cast. "What else?"

"A cut on my leg. A couple of stitches on the side of my head."

"Because someone attacked you?"

"In a manner of speaking, but—"

"Where was your partner?"

"Doing his job."

"Apparently he wasn't, or you wouldn't have been hurt."

"If Ryan had been the one in back of the building, he'd be the one in the cast." At least, that's what she kept telling herself. She didn't want to consider the possibility that Red had gone after her because he thought he could overpower her. "I'm a good cop, Mason. I can handle myself. Don't start playing macho with me, acting like you think I need some guy to protect me or we're going to have a real problem."

Mason held up both hands. "Sorry. That's not what I meant. It's just hard to see you that way. I shouldn't…"

Shouldn't what? Shouldn't care? That's not what she wanted. But she was back to that same old dilemma that kept circling her mind—the one that defeated her every time it came up. How *did* Ryan and Eisley and the other married guys walk the line between their personal and professional lives? The idea that she might have to spend the rest of her life alone filled her with sadness.

"I overreacted," she said. "That whole subject is a touchy one for me right now."

Mason smiled and leaned over to kiss her as if it were something he did all the time. "You want to talk about it?"

She shook her head and held on to the feeling of his lips on hers so she could remember it later. "It's nothing. My boss has a tough time with women on the force, and he's busting my chops right now. But it's okay. I can handle him."

"He's busting your chops because you're a woman?"

"That's my take."

"Can't you go over his head? I thought gender bias was illegal."

"It is, but trust me, complaining will only make things worse. Even the guys who are okay with women in the ranks get edgy when we start flinging the gender card around. It's far better to just take your lumps and prove yourself."

"How many lumps are you expected to take?"

She grinned. "Twice as many as a man. Piece of cake."

Mason was laughing when he bent to kiss her again. When he pulled away, he was serious. He cupped her cheek in his hand and traced a slow pattern with his thumb while his eyes searched hers. She had no idea what he was looking for, but she hoped desperately she had the right answers.

As the pain medication began to cloud her mind and heat curled slowly through her, she gave up even trying to think and pressed her face against his hand. It felt so good to sit with him like this, and somewhere beneath the pleasant haze of the medication, she realized that she wanted much more of this.

"How's the pain? Is the pill starting to take effect?"

"I think so. I don't feel anything at the moment."

"Is it going to make you loopy?"

She laughed. "Most likely."

"Want me to help you into bed?"

She looked into his eyes, too far gone to worry about the secrets hidden behind them. "You must have read my mind."

She saw him swallow, saw the desire in his face, and felt almost giddy when she realized she was responsible for it. He leaned close again and covered her mouth with his, brushing her lips lightly with his tongue until she opened her mouth and invited him in. He put his arms around her slowly, careful not to jostle her and treating her with such exquisite care, she felt a lump form in her throat.

"Much as I'd like that," he whispered when they came up for air, "I'm not the kind of guy who takes advantage of a woman who's higher than a kite."

"I'm not that high," she protested.

He pulled away and helped her to her feet. "No. Not now."

He helped her down the hall with a gentleness that almost took away the sting of his rejection. "I'm going to take your keys so I can lock up behind me," he said as he sat her on the foot of the bed. "I'll bring them back on my way to work in the morning."

"Isn't Debra still suspended from school?" Her voice sounded thick and slurred, like someone about to go down for the count.

Mason nodded and pulled back the covers on her bed. "I took today off work, but the crew ran into trouble again pulling out the sprinkling system. I'm going to have to be there for at least half the day tomorrow."

"What about Debra?"

"I'm just going to have to take her with me."

"Oh, but you can't do that. She'll be miserable."

"She's been suspended from school."

Mason picked up her pillow and fluffed it. "She might have to suffer just a little."

Jolene pulled in a breath, trying to catch the muted spice scent he wore. She hoped her pillow smelled like him now. "I'm not saying that I think she should…" the word escaped her. Her head felt light, almost as if it were no longer attached to her body. She lay across the foot of the bed, her good arm under her head, and tried to focus on what she wanted to tell him. "I was just thinking that since I'm home and she's home, and you need to work…That's all I was saying."

She didn't hear him moving, but suddenly he was standing over her, smiling as if something funny had happened. "You're offering to watch Debra while I work?"

"What's the matter, don't you trust me?"

He bent and slid one arm under her shoulders. "I can't ask you to do that. It's going above and beyond."

"But you're my friend." Her eyes felt heavy, and she had the strong urge to close them, but she didn't want to fall asleep. She might miss something. "I can do it. Really I can. We can talk about drugs and stuff. Just set my alarm. Five o'clock, okay?"

She heard him laugh—at least she thought she did. She couldn't be sure because she was suddenly standing beside him with her head on his shoulder. Or maybe she was leaning on him. All she could hear was the steady beat of his heart. Steady. That described Mason, all right. Rock solid, even if he did have a few issues. It would be so easy to fall in love with him.

He murmured something, but she was too far gone to know what it was. She thought he helped her lie down, even thought he pulled the covers up over her. She felt his mouth on hers again, but she wasn't sure if that was real or a dream. She could feel his breath on her cheek, warm and comforting, and his voice, low and sexy in her ear. "It would be easy to fall in love with you, too. I'll see you in the morning."

CHAPTER TWENTY

NOT AT ALL SURE which parts of last night had been real and which had been a dream, Jolene dragged herself out of bed when her alarm went off at five the next morning. By six, she was cleaned up and dressed. She didn't look perky, but at least she didn't look as though she'd been rolled in soy sauce and chicken lo mein.

Now that she was conscious and thinking clearly—sort of—she wondered what she'd been thinking. No food had magically appeared in her cupboards overnight. No milk, no fruit, no veggies. No cereal. Even her mother would be hard-pressed to pull a decent meal out of this kitchen, but dragging Debra down to Burger King for breakfast wasn't the answer.

At the top of her to-do list today was a trip to the grocery store. And then what? For the first time in weeks, she had the urge to call her mother. Margaret would know what to tell her. She'd have some simple recipe for muffins or some terrific egg thing that even Jolene could throw together. But what kind of person would that make her, calling to beg for help with a recipe after barely speaking to her mother for nearly a month? She couldn't do that, so she did the next best thing and dug through cupboards and the last few unpacked boxes to unearth the cookbook her mother gave her for Christmas a few years back.

She knew next to nothing about kids. Kids who weren't riding in the back of a police car. Except that was exactly how she'd met Debra.

The doorbell rang at exactly six-fifteen. Rock-solid, steady Mason, showing up right on time…with Debra.

Smiling as if she weren't in a panic, Jolene invited them both inside. Mason, tall, dark, freshly showered, incredibly handsome. Debra, wearing baggy pants and an oversize hooded sweatshirt. Strangely enough, her curiosity actually seemed stronger this morning than her determination to look bored and unhappy.

Before Jolene could even blink, Mason returned her keys, promised to call later and left, pleading the time. Debra slumped into the living room on a pair of Fila shoes—laced, not tied—and tossed a thick notebook and a couple of pens onto the coffee table. Jolene hoped that meant she'd brought schoolwork.

Debra took a long look around. "So this is your apartment?"

"It is." Jolene closed the door behind them. "And you're staying here with me today?"

Debra nodded, but her chin stuck out in that way it did when she felt challenged. "Dad said you asked."

"I did," Jolene said quickly. "You might be sorry, though. There's not much to do."

"That's okay. I'd rather stare at the walls than dig holes and plant flowers all day."

"First rule," Jolene said. "No trashing your dad. If that's what you plan to do, maybe you'd better go dig holes and plant flowers instead. I'm not going to listen to it."

"You're on *his* side?"

"I'm not on any side," Jolene said, heading

for the coffeemaker. "And you know what? There shouldn't be a side to take."

Debra's shoes made a *slop-slop* noise on the linoleum as she trailed after her. "You like my dad, don't you?"

Jolene wasn't sure what to say to that. To begin with she didn't know what she and Mason had and would Debra accept a relationship between them if there was one? Or would she wig out the way she had over her mother's marriage? But Debra was waiting for an answer.

"I do like him," she admitted. "He's a great guy."

Debra sneered. "If you're not his daughter."

Jolene could see how hard Mason was trying with his daughter, so the girl's stubborn refusal to give even an inch made no sense. "What's wrong with him, Debra? What does he do that's so awful?"

"For one thing, he made me come here."

"Here? To my house? I hardly think that's cruel and unusual punishment."

"Not *here*. I mean Tulsa. And he's making me stay for six months."

Jolene shook her head in confusion.

"Back up a bit. I thought it was your idea to come here. Or your mother's. As for why he wants you to stay, he wants to spend time with you. Is that such an awful thing?"

Debra collapsed into a chair at the dining table and dropped her chin onto her hands. "That's what he says, but it's not true. All he wants to do is spend time at work and yell at me for not going to diving practice and stuff."

"He spends a lot of time at work?"

"He leaves this early every morning. I have to get myself ready for school and catch the bus. He doesn't get home until after seven every night, and he's hardly ever home on weekends. What do you think?"

This was the most Jolene had ever heard from Debra, and she prayed she wouldn't do or say the wrong thing. She leaned into the corner of the cupboards. "Yeah, he works a lot. My parents always worked long hours, too. But I had my brother to hang out with, so that made a difference."

"It's not great when you're alone."

"No, I'll bet it's not. Have you talked to your dad?"

"Sort of."

"What does *sort of* mean?"

"He doesn't want to talk about it. He just says he has to work that much or we won't have anything."

"Well, it is tough when you run your own business," Jolene agreed.

"Not that tough. Ike says he's obsessed and trying not to be like his dad."

"Really?" Interesting. "When did Ike say that?" And why would he say something like that in front of Debra?

Debra shrugged and glanced around. "I heard them arguing about it once at Ike's house. You got any bread and eggs? My mom taught me how to make French toast. I could make us some."

"I'm afraid not. We need to make a run to the grocery store before we do anything." Jolene chewed the inside of her lip. "Do you have any idea what Ike meant by that?"

"By what? Oh. Sorry. No, but my dad was pretty mad and after that I didn't think it would be such a good idea to tell him I think he works too much."

"No. I can see why you wouldn't. But on the other hand, if he doesn't know how you feel, how can he address it?"

"He doesn't want to anyway, so it's no big deal."

"You know what, Debra? You say that a lot, but I don't think you mean it. I think it's a very big deal to you, so why is it so hard to tell your dad that you really love him and want him to pay more attention to you?"

Debra furrowed her brows and pushed to her feet. "The last thing I want is for him to pay more attention to me. He's mad at me all the time already."

"I'm not talking about the kind of attention where you're in trouble," Jolene said, still trying to keep the tone casual. "If you could pick, what's something you'd like your dad to do with you?"

"I don't know. Nothing."

"You wanted to go to the Cherokee Center yesterday, and he took you there."

"No, I wanted him to tell me about my grandparents. He took me there instead. Like finding out about a bunch of people who got moved onto a reservation a hundred years ago is going to tell me anything."

Jolene left the safety of her corner and sat at the table with Debra. "If it helps at all, he won't talk to me, either. There's something about your grandparents that upsets him, though, that's for sure."

Debra made a face. "You think?"

Jolene grinned and propped her broken arm on the table. "Whatever it is, I don't think he's keeping some big secret just to make you feel bad. It's not about you, it's about him."

"So?"

"So maybe you and I should both try understanding that whatever it is, he needs to work through a few things before he can tell us about it. We all have stuff we're trying to sort through. I've got family things, and you've got your mom with and her husband."

Debra slumped down in her chair and rolled her eyes. "Bill."

"Right. Bill. But the point is, just because somebody else wants us to get everything all lined up and worked out right away, that doesn't mean it's going to happen that way. You might really want your dad to be able to tell you about your grandparents, but he can't do it yet."

"You don't get it."

"Oh, but I do. My parents had something they couldn't tell me for thirty years. When I finally found out about it, I got really upset.

I thought they were selfish and…well, a bunch of other stuff. But maybe they were just confused like your dad."

"They kept a secret from you for thirty years?"

"Yeah. Long time. Not fun." Jolene stood and grabbed her keys. "What do you say we head to the store? I'm starving."

With a shrug, Debra got to her feet. "I thought your leg was hurt. How can you drive?"

The question brought Jolene up short. If she were by herself, she wouldn't hesitate. Her leg felt much better this morning, and Albertson's was only a few blocks away. But she really shouldn't take the risk of driving with Debra in the car. "We'll take a cab."

"Are you serious? Isn't that expensive?"

"Not as expensive as an accident would be." Jolene had no idea if she'd made any headway with Debra, but she hoped so. For her sake and for Mason's.

Fifteen minutes later they were buckled into the backseat of a taxi and rolling along Memorial Drive in the pre-rush-hour traffic. Debra seemed almost excited by the adventure.

"So how long do you have to be off work?" she asked.

"At least a week."

"I guess we're both on suspension, huh?"

Jolene laughed. "Yeah, I guess we are."

Debra watched a couple of homeless people pushing a shopping cart along the sidewalk. "Do you like being a cop?"

"Yes I do. A lot."

"Why?"

These were easy questions. Jolene had been answering them for so long, she didn't even have to think about them. "I like helping people. I'd like the world to be a safe place, where people can leave their homes without worry. Being a cop is my way of making that happen."

"Even if you get hurt?"

"It's a risk," she admitted. "We all know that something can happen when we're out there on duty, but we try to be careful, and for the most part we're very safe. Still sometimes accidents happen, just like anywhere else."

"Did the guy who did this want to hurt you?"

Jolene shook her head slowly. "I don't

think so. Not really. What he wanted was to protect himself. I just happened to get in his way."

Debra frowned. "That means he wanted to hurt you. It wasn't an accident."

"No," Jolene said. "It wasn't an accident."

"Is that why you don't have any kids? Because your job is so dangerous?"

Nothing like a nice, blunt question. Jolene wasn't in the habit of sharing personal details of her life with people, but Mason was so closed off about his past, she didn't have the heart to tell Debra the answer to that question was none of her business. She glanced at the taxi driver, hoping he wasn't listening. "It's one of the reasons."

"Does that mean you're never going to get married?"

Jolene tried to smile. "I don't know, Debra. I never gave it much thought. Nobody knows what's around the next corner."

"Would you marry my dad if he asked you?"

"Okay, now," Jolene said with a laugh, "that's far enough. Your dad and I are friends, that's all."

"That's not all," Debra said, rolling her eyes. "I see the way you look at each other."

"All right, so maybe we're a little more than friends."

"He'll probably ask you," Debra said decisively. "That's just the way my luck goes."

"I take it that means that you wouldn't be happy if he did?"

The cab pulled up in front of the store, and Debra shrugged. "I wouldn't care. It would be okay, I guess, as long as you didn't yell at me to get out of bed or tell me to leave my mom alone when I need her help with homework."

Jolene paid the driver, and they spent the next few minutes finding a cart and sorting out which of them would push. "Tell me about Bill," she said when they were rolling through the produce department.

Debra spotted a container filled with cut-up melon and held it up for approval. Jolene nodded. "Ever since he came along, he acts like he owns my mom or something. And all the stuff we used to do together, we don't do anymore. Either Bill doesn't like Thai food or Bill doesn't have time or Bill needs to work or Bill wants to dig the lint out from between his toes or something."

Jolene laughed as she added a small bag of oranges to the cart. "Something tells me Bill's toe lint has never really been a topic of conversation between you and your mom."

"No, but just about everything else is. She thinks he's so-o-o perfect. Whatever Bill wants, that's what we do."

"Ah. I see." Jolene added lettuce, green onions and tomatoes and looked around for the salad dressing. "It became your job to adjust."

"Yep."

"And that's no fun," Jolene commiserated. "I mean, we all know when someone new comes along, there's some adjusting."

"Bill didn't have to. We had to move into his house, so I had to go to a new school. I lost all my friends, and my bedroom, and Bill doesn't want me to put posters on my walls or anything."

Jolene slowed her pace and looked down at the top of Debra's head. No wonder the poor thing was miserable. So she left that environment and came to Tulsa, where she started adjusting all over again. "Does your dad know about all this?"

"I don't know. I don't think he cares."

"Of course he cares, Debra. More than you know. He gets things wrong sometimes, but he doesn't do it on purpose. He just makes a mistake. Everybody makes them—even you."

A flush crept into Debra's cheeks. "You're talking about the drug stuff, aren't you? But I'm not doing drugs. Really I'm not. I'm just—" She shook her head. "I'm just messing around, that's all."

Jolene spotted the salad dressings one aisle over and started moving in that direction. "And trying to make your dad mad?"

"No. I'm not trying to make him mad. I don't like it when people are mad at me."

Jolene slipped an arm around Debra's shoulders and gave her a squeeze. "Well, sweetie, if that's the case, you're going about it the wrong way. I wish you could see what drugs do to people. I see it every day, and it's heartbreaking. Before I got hurt, I had to interview a mother whose son lives on the streets, never takes a bath, stinks, scares people and steals money from his own parents. If you don't want people to be mad at you, playing around with drugs is *not* the way to go."

"I'm not going to use drugs," Debra said quietly.

"Are you trying to see what your dad will do if you're in trouble? You think he'll just pack you up and ship you off again?"

Debra said, "No," in that tone of voice that really means yes.

"Do you really want to go back?"

"Yes. No." She kicked a metal shelf and said, "Ever since Bill came along, my mom yells at me for no reason, just because I have my stereo on or talk on the phone or watch TV."

"I take it Bill also likes things quiet."

"He can't stand noise."

That must make life rough with a teenager around—especially one who liked to rattle the walls with her CDs. "Does your mom mind the noise?"

"She didn't used to. She used to come into my room and sing and do this dorky dance, but now all she does is yell at me to turn it down."

"What about your dad? What does he do?"

"Sometimes he asks me to turn it down."

"Does he yell at you?"

Debra seemed reluctant to admit it, but she shook her head. "No."

"One mark in the good-guy column."

Debra smiled grudgingly. "Yeah, I guess he's okay about that."

Jolene felt so encouraged, she not only bought the makings for French toast, but she decided to take a chance on pancakes, as well. The directions on the back of the muffin mix didn't look so hard…

By the time they called for a cab and wheeled the cart outside, Jolene had more groceries than her apartment had seen since she moved in. Probably more than she'd ever bought at one time. Her mother would be so proud.

But they weren't even halfway back to her apartment when the bottom fell out of the fantasy world. One minute the cab was idling at a stoplight while she and Debra laughed over some song lyrics on the radio. The next, she found herself looking at a large man in filthy khakis and a plaid shirt. He was on the other side of the road, too far away for her to be sure it was Red, but the thick red hair hanging in greasy waves to his shoulders looked familiar, and he limped slightly—as someone might if he'd taken a tumble down a set of stairs a few nights ago.

She lunged forward to get the cab driver's attention. "Slow down. Turn around and drive back along the street slowly." She sat back and dialed Ryan's number on her cell phone. "I want you to lie down on the seat, Debra, and don't sit up until I tell you it's okay."

The cab driver took so long finding a place to turn around, Jolene was ready to jump out of her skin. Ryan's cell phone rang four times before he bothered to answer.

"Hey, Jo-Jo. What's this? It's not seven o'clock in the morning. I don't even get up this early, and I'm still punching the clock. I thought you were supposed to be taking it easy."

"Well wake up, because I found him."

"Who?"

"I'm watching Big Red walk down Memorial Drive."

"Where?"

She craned to see the coordinates and rattled them off. "Come on, Ryan. If he leaves the street, I'm going to lose him. There's no way I'll be able to follow him on foot."

"Has he seen you?"

"Not yet. I'm in a cab. He's not paying much attention."

"Okay. I'm on my way. Call in and get some uniforms on the way. I don't want him getting another shot at you while you're alone."

"I'm fine," she snarled. But she wasn't fine at all. She had one arm in a cast, a leg that was already aching from pushing a shopping cart around a grocery store and, worst of all, a child lying on the seat beside her.

They drew abreast of Big Red and the cab driver slammed on his brakes. Jolene shouted at him to get going, but it was too late. Red saw her and vaulted over a hanging chain barricade. Before she could even think of a way to stop him, he'd disappeared behind the building. "Is there an alley? Can we get behind these buildings?"

"I don't know, lady. I don't think so."

"Well, could you *try?* This is a police matter. It's urgent."

The cabbie stepped on the gas, and they shot toward the end of the block, but Red was gone by the time they found the alley—

and the worst part was, Jolene wasn't entirely sure whether she was frustrated, angry… or relieved.

CHAPTER TWENTY-ONE

THE REST OF THE DAY passed uneventfully. Ryan took over the search for Big Red and sent Jolene home. She might have argued if Debra hadn't been with her. But she couldn't very well send Debra off by herself in the cab, so she swallowed her objections. At home, she made herself stay busy with household chores, hoping they would keep her from thinking about the job, leaving Debra to fend for herself.

While Jolene started a load of laundry, Debra put away the groceries. Then Jolene skimmed through her cookbook, as Debra worked on the report for her history class. By the time Mason called to say he was on his way home at a few minutes after seven, Jolene was even more convinced that Debra felt displaced in her mother's life and wasn't convinced she belonged in her father's.

When Mason arrived, he invited Jolene to join them for dinner at their favorite Mexican restaurant. Debra seemed almost eager for her to join them, and even seemed to enjoy herself as she told Mason about seeing Big Red and their half-hearted attempt to chase him by taxi. And when Mason invited Jolene to come up to their apartment afterward, Jolene didn't even hesitate.

Debra had spent the day separated from her stereo, so it didn't take long for her to shut herself away and start the music. Mason joined Jolene on the couch and pulled her into the crook of his arm as if they sat together after a shared meal every day of the week.

"I had a good time with Debra today," she told him. "I hope you'll let her come back tomorrow."

He gave her a look that made her think about kissing in the moonlight. "Are you sure you feel up to it?"

"Absolutely. My arm hasn't hurt much today, and my leg feels a lot better. And believe it or not, Debra was a real help."

"I'm glad to hear it."

"We had a good talk this morning," she

said, shifting again so she could see into his eyes. "Did you know she thinks you work too much? She's behaving the way she is because she wants your attention."

"She has my attention," Mason said with a humorless laugh. "And she's getting more of it every day."

"I don't see you sitting down for a heart-to-heart talk with her, or even sitting in the same space and watching a movie."

Mason's eyes clouded. "I've tried having a heart-to-heart with her, Jolene. She's even less interested in sitting here with me and watching a movie. She'd rather be in there, listening to her stereo."

"That's what she says about you. Not the stereo part, but she doesn't think you're interested in talking to her. She doesn't think she's important to you."

"That's ridiculous. She knows she's important."

"Does she?" Jolene knew she was in dangerous territory, but she cared too much about Mason and Debra to remain silent. "While you were gone today, she was like a different person. She even offered to help fold my laundry. She only used her portable CD player once, and then only for about fifteen minutes."

"I'm well aware she'd rather be any-where but here—"

"That's not what I'm saying, and I don't think it's true. Stop and think about it for a minute. She used to be number one in her mother's life, and then Bill came along. Now she's not only been bumped from there, she's here with you and coming in second fiddle to your job."

"She said that?"

"Not in so many words. She told me you still haven't answered any of her questions about her grandparents. What are you so afraid of?"

Mason shook his head. "Too many things to list."

Jolene watched him for a minute and wished desperately that things could be easier between them. "Were you embar-rassed by your parents, Mason? Is that it?"

He laughed sharply and stood. "Embar-rassed? You have no idea."

"Why? What did they do?"

His eyes flashed with fury. "Why is it so important to you?"

"I care about you. And about Debra. I want to know because it's eating you up inside, but whatever happened with your parents makes no difference to me. It's not going to change who you are, and it's not going to change how I feel, but if you're not careful it is going to cost your relationship with your daughter."

Mason looked away. "She'll forget about all of this once she's finished her report."

"If you think that, you're really not paying attention." Jolene hated feeling at a disadvantage, so she stood and put herself at his level. "You keep saying how important Debra is to you. If you mean that, stop worrying about how you feel and pay attention to what she needs."

He stared at her for a long moment, so still that the only sign of life was the rise and fall of his chest as he breathed. Jolene watched emotions crossing his face, and she wished she knew what he was thinking. When he finally spoke, his voice was so low she could barely hear him. "That was a low blow, Jolene. How will admitting that my mother was a whore make my daughter's life better?"

That knocked the wind out of Jolene's lungs. She sat again, landing hard against the cushions.

He sank onto the couch beside her, but he kept his gaze on his hands. "My father was a drifter. From one job to another, one bottle to another, one woman to another." He glanced up at her, almost daring her to pull away.

Jolene kept her face impassive.

"I don't know why he bothered to marry my mother. Sometime later, I came along. The old man was gone by then. Moved on to greener pastures, I guess. He came by to see us a few times, though, because I remember following him around the yard, wishing he'd talk to me."

Jolene could have sworn her heart broke, but she tried not to show it. Mason wouldn't want pity.

"But he didn't?"

"He was after money. That's all he ever wanted. And my mother usually had a little." The memories made him too jumpy to sit, so he paced to the other side of the room and stared out into the parking lot. "I don't know when she started, but I was about six when

I noticed an unusual number of male visitors stopping by the house. It didn't take much longer to figure out that's why my mother never left the house to work."

His pain was so raw Jolene could almost feel it. She knew he was watching her for anything he could read as a negative reaction. "Do you know why she did it? Was it because your dad left?"

Mason shook his head. "She was an alcoholic. My dad couldn't hold a candle to her when it came to the bottle. Welcoming male visitors didn't require any special skill, she didn't have to work when she didn't feel like it, and most of her clients didn't care whether she was drunk or sober. It was the perfect job for her."

"You must have hated it."

"I hated it, and I hated her. I learned how to fend for myself at a very young age. I was cooking hot dogs by the time I was six, and I made a mean bowl of soup by seven. Most of the time, the only food there was I'd stolen from the reservation store."

He wasn't the first child Jolene had run into who'd been neglected, and he wouldn't be the last, but that didn't make it any easier to hear. "Why didn't someone take you out of there? Didn't you have family?"

"A grandmother, dying of cancer. She's the only family I know of." He smiled half-heartedly. "I'm not like you, Jolene. Your big problem is not knowing what to do with two families. Mine is that I didn't even have one."

"You had Henry, and he cared for you a lot."

"I had Henry." Mason ran a hand along the back of his neck. "Thank God for Henry. Without him, I don't know how I might have turned out."

"You went to live with him when you were eight?"

He nodded. "Some idiot let my mother borrow a car. I guess she'd run out of booze or something. Anyway, she was on her way home from the city, but she never made it. It was a couple of days before anybody thought to come looking for me."

"Oh, Mason. All that time you were by yourself? You must've been so frightened."

"I didn't matter a whole lot to the folks on the reservation. When they finally remembered me, they fought about who was going to take me. Nobody wanted Mary Black-fox's kid around their children."

And that's why he turned his back on his heritage. "That had to hurt. It's no wonder you didn't want anything to do with them."

"They had no use for me. I had no use for them." Mason rose from the couch and moved away from her. Leaning one shoulder against the wall he looked her in the eye. "So now you know."

"So what are you afraid of, Mason? That Debra's going to lose respect for you if she knows the truth?"

"She doesn't respect me now. There's not a whole lot to lose, is there?" When he spoke again, he tempered his sharp tone. "Maybe I'm just afraid she'll start seeing me as Mary Blackfox's kid."

"The one who wasn't good enough for anybody to love?"

"That's the one."

"You're also Ike's brother, my friend, an astute businessman, a gifted landscape artist and an incredibly sexy man, not to mention Debra's father…"

"Yeah, but it's Mary Blackfox's son I can't get away from."

"You don't need to get away from it. No one cares about that except you."

"Yeah. But I *do* care, that's the thing. You're Billy Starr's daughter. I'm Mary Blackfox's kid."

"But when you stay focused on that, you're just about guaranteeing that's all anybody else will ever see. There's so much more to you, Mason. Let people see that."

He shook his head slowly. "I look at Debra flirting with drugs and all I can see is my mother falling down drunk, ruining every holiday, every birthday, every occasion. That kind of addictive personality runs in families, and I've passed it down to my daughter. How do you think that makes me feel?"

"You haven't sealed her fate. The choice is hers. You'll do more for her by helping her understand why she needs to be so careful than you will by shutting her out."

"Shutting her out?" Mason laughed softly and lifted his face toward the ceiling. "My God, that's what I've been doing, isn't it? Just like my old man did with me."

Jolene got to her feet and closed the distance between them. She touched his shoulder gently, and when he didn't pull away or stiffen beneath her fingers, she slid her arms beneath his and leaned her head against his chest. "You're a great guy, Mason. I wish you could believe that."

Very slowly, his arms tightened around her and he leaned his cheek against the top of her head. "Maybe I will one of these days if you stick around and keep reminding me."

It was the closest thing to a commitment Jolene had ever come up against, and it made her unbelievably nervous. How could she make promises she might not be able to keep, especially to someone who needed consistency so badly?

She drew away gently, hoping he wouldn't think she was reacting to Mary Blackfox's kid. "Let's not worry about the future," she said. "We both have enough to worry about today." Needing to clear her head, she leaned and kissed him quickly. "It's getting late. I should go."

"You can't walk home. Let me drive you."

"It's just across the parking lot."

"That's still too far."

He started toward her but she held up her good hand. "No, Mason. Please. Stay here. I'm really not an invalid. I'll be okay."

She shut the door behind her, wondering how long it would be before that last part was actually true.

WHEN HE STILL hadn't heard from Jolene by the following evening, Mason found himself in a foul, foul mood. He was doing his best not to take it out on Debra, but he was afraid she was getting some of the fall-out in spite of his best efforts. It wasn't fair, and he wasn't proud of himself, but he wasn't a saint and he'd never claimed to be a perfect father. Just one who was willing to try hard. Maybe not hard enough.

He'd burned the hamburger for dinner, dripped grease onto a burner and damn near set the apartment on fire, and now he was standing in his open doorway freezing his butt off and trying to wave at least some of the smoke outside. The rap music pounding from Debra's bedroom did nothing to make him feel better.

He should never have told Jolene the truth about his family. The horrified look on her face when he'd confessed had not only been hard on his ego, it had been downright humiliating. What made it all worse was that he knew she had feelings for him—at least he thought she did. If not, then she was a better actress than he'd given her credit for.

But did she love him? Until that moment in the living room, he'd have said yes. Now, he realized how wrong he'd been.

Forget her, he told himself as he watched smoke billow out into the night. Forget the deep caramel-brown of her eyes, the gold shimmer hidden in her dark hair, the soft curve of her cheek and the oh-so-satisfying swell of her hip. Forget the fact that she cared more about Debra than anyone except her mother—and there were times when he wondered about Alex. Forget the fact that he felt more comfortable with her than he did with any other human being, or that he could talk to her about anything.

Forget all that and just count yourself lucky that she didn't lead you on indefinitely.

But when the phone rang and he nearly broke a leg trying to get to it, he had to admit that maybe he didn't want to forget about her. At least not yet.

"Mason? Oh, I'm so glad I caught you. I thought for sure you'd be out somewhere."

Alex. He sat on the arm of the couch and tried not to sound disappointed. "Why would you think that?"

"Debra told me you've been seeing someone. Is it serious?"

His "relationship" with Jolene was the last thing he wanted to discuss with Alexandra. "Not exactly. Sorry to disappoint you.'

She gave a little laugh and moved on as if the subject hadn't really interested her at all. "Oh, I'm not disappointed. I just thought it was nice, that's all. It's really time that you got a life of your own. Something other than work, that is."

"Fun as it is to talk about my love life with you, you want me to call Debra?"

"Not yet. How's she doing with the suspension?"

"Surprisingly, not bad. She spent yesterday at the Cultural Center, and the day before she went with me to the job site. I put her to work hauling decorative bark chips in a wheelbarrow."

Alex laughed. "I'll bet she loved that."

"She didn't complain as much as I thought she would. I talked to the school district this afternoon. She should be able to go back to school on Monday."

"That's good, Mason. I'm glad. I wasn't really sure about this arrangement when I sent her to stay with you, but I just didn't know what to do. I have to admit, I think you've been good for her.

The compliment surprised him. "Thanks, but it's not just me. My friend—Jolene—has done a lot to help, too."

"This is the woman you're not serious about?"

"It's the woman who isn't serious about me," Mason admitted. "The story of my life."

"I was serious about you," Alex protested. "I just had trouble with Debra and me always being second place with you. I even understood why you were so driven to succeed. Except I needed more than you could give me."

"Well, at least I'm not repeating the same old mistake over and over again. Jolene seems to need a whole lot less time than I'm willing to give."

"I'm sorry. Truly. I'm not just saying that."

She sounded sincere. "Thanks. It doesn't help but it's nice to hear."

She laughed softly. "I'm glad we've been able to put the past behind us, Mason. It's good for Debra's sake that we can get along."

"Yeah. Me, too."

"I guess I'd better warn you why I'm calling."

The smile slipped from his face. "You're calling to take Debra back?"

"No. Relax. I promised you six months, and you'll have them. I have some news for her, but I don't think she's going to be happy about it."

"What kind of news?"

"Bill and I are expecting a baby. Debra's going to be a big sister."

"That's great, Alex. I know you must be thrilled."

"I am, but I'm also worried about Debra. She had such a tough time sharing me with Bill, I just don't know whether this will push her off the deep end. What do you think?

Mason shrugged and glanced toward his daughter's door. "She's a little calmer now than she was. We actually have conversations now and then, and less than half of them involve screaming. She might not take it as hard as you think. When's the baby due?"

Alex hesitated just long enough to rouse his suspicions, and when she answered, she confirmed them. "In September."

"So you were already pregnant when you sent her to live with me."

"Yes."

"Is that why you sent her away?"

"Don't say it like that! I sent her to stay with you because I felt like death warmed over all the time. She and Bill couldn't be in the same room for five minutes without a fight, and I simply couldn't deal with them."

He watched the last, frail wisps of smoke drifting out of the open door. "You should have told her the truth, Alex."

"And let her think I sent her away because of the baby?"

"She's not stupid. She'll figure it out anyway."

"Maybe so, but at least I feel better now. If she gets upset, I can talk with her. Reason with her."

He thought about the pain he'd seen on Jolene's face when she told him about her mother's lie. "The trouble with that is, she'll be so focused on the lie she won't hear what you're saying. There's no excuse you can give her that will make up for lying to her in the first place."

"She's a child. She doesn't need to know every little thing."

"I wouldn't call a brand new brother or sister a little thing, would you?"

Alex's voice grew tight and tense. "That's not what I meant and you know it. I need you to work with me, Mason, not against me. Please don't tell her this is something she needs to be upset about."

A knot of tension tightened in his neck, and he rubbed the spot in a vain attempt to get rid of it. "I'm not working against you, Alex. And I'm not planning to influence Debra's reaction, so relax. Just don't be surprised if she's more upset about the lie than about the baby, that's all I'm saying."

"Right. Well, we might as well get this over with. Get her on, okay?"

He put the phone down and walked slowly down the hall. He wasn't looking forward to the next few days, and he couldn't help being a little annoyed with Alex for choosing tonight to tell Debra. Just when things had started looking up.

Give thanks for all the opportunities to

grow a little each day, he told himself. But today, he would have been a whole lot more thankful without the opportunities he'd been given.

HE WAS SITTING at the kitchen table nursing his second cup of coffee the next morning when Debra came in, hair tousled, eyes puffy. She stood just inside the door, her arms crossed. "Did she tell you?"

"Who? Your mother?"

She nodded, looking glum. "About the baby?"

"She told me." He set his cup on the table and shifted in his chair so he could see her better. "What do you think?"

"I think it's stupid. She's too old to be having babies, isn't she?"

"Not exactly." He grinned. "She has a few more good years left."

"You mean she could have another one?"

"I suppose she could. Would that bother you?"

She flounced toward the cupboard, glaring at him as if he'd just announced that the world was flat. "Well, duh! Of course it would bother me. First she ships me off here, then she starts having babies. Bill's babies. She's going to forget all about me."

"I don't think that's going to happen." Mason assured her.

She pulled a box of Marshmallow Puffies from the cupboard and reached for a bowl. "What makes you so sure?"

"Well, just look at you. You're a great kid. You're smart, and you're funny—when you want to be. You're a strong diver, and you're pretty darn cute to boot. How could anybody forget about you?"

Her eyes narrowed into a sharp accusation. "You did.'

"Not true. I never forgot about you."

"That's a lie."

"No, it's the truth." Mason opened the fridge and pulled out the milk. "I might not have been the world's greatest dad, but I always loved you."

Debra scowled at him, but she stopped arguing that point and switched to another. "What's she doing having babies, anyway? That's just gross. We're learning about it in health class, and it's disgusting."

Not the talk Mason had been gearing up for all night, but maybe he should have been.

Any dad with a half a brain would figure that talk about babies and pregnancy would lead straight back to sex, wouldn't he? "They've taught you all about it, huh?"

"Not all about it." Debra carried her breakfast to the table and dropped heavily into a chair. "Just enough for me to know that I never want to do it."

Mason ducked his head so she wouldn't see his grin. "Never?"

"Never."

He took a minute to compose himself. "You know, I don't think there's a dad in the world that wouldn't take a few victory laps if he heard his daughter say that, but in the interest of fairness I probably ought to warn you that someday you'll change your mind."

She brushed a stray hair from her forehead as she splashed milk into the bowl. "No, I won't."

"Okay. Fine. Frankly, I'm good with that. But if you ever do change you mind, be smart, okay? Did they talk to you about protection?"

"Like condoms?" She made a face and nodded.

"Something like that. Twelve is far too

young for any of that, by the way." He sipped coffee and added, "So is thirteen. And fourteen. And…"

Debra scooped up a spoonful of cereal and eyed him. "Do you ever do it?"

He spit out a mouthful of coffee and stared at her in disbelief. "Did you just ask me if I have sex?"

"Well, do you?"

"No. Not recently. Not that it's something I'm comfortable talking about with my kid."

"If you did, would you use protection?"

"Yes."

"If you did, would it be with Jolene?"

Mason stood abruptly. "Okay, conversation over."

"Does that mean yes?"

"It means this isn't a conversation I'm going to have with my twelve-year-old daughter." He poured the rest of his coffee down the sink and opened the kitchen blind to let the sun in. "Hurry and get dressed so we're not late."

"But you like her, don't you."

"I like her a lot, but that still doesn't mean I'm going to discuss this with you. We're supposed to be talking about you and how you feel about your mom being pregnant."

"I already told you, it's gross."

"Maybe you won't think that once you get home and see the baby."

She slurped up another mouthful of cereal and answered with her mouth full. "I'm not going home," she said. At least that's what Mason thought she said. It wasn't easy to tell around all the Marshmallow Puffies.

"Well, not until November or so, but—"

"I'm not going home at all," Debra said with a bob of her head to show that she meant business. "I'm staying here. With you. Forever."

JOLENE COULD HARDLY breathe as she made the long walk from the street to Thea High Eagle's door the next evening. A light rain had fallen earlier, and now puddles lined the sidewalks and the lights shimmered in the moist air. Her heart hammered, and a thousand thoughts raced through her mind.

Maybe she should wait until tomorrow. Maybe she should call first. Wouldn't that be the polite thing to do? Probably. But if she didn't go knock on that door now, she might never find the courage. She'd put this off for so long, she wasn't even sure what to say.

Her stomach lurched as she climbed the steps, and she could have sworn her heart stopped beating entirely as she pressed the doorbell. From inside the house, she heard the bell peal. In just seconds her life would change forever. She knew it as certainly as she knew that the moon was climbing in the night sky and the day would dawn tomorrow.

After only a few seconds, the door opened and Thea stood in front of her. She looked surprised, then wary. "*Osiyo*. It's Jolene, isn't it? Am I remembering right?"

Jolene had rehearsed what she wanted to say a dozen times on the way across town, but getting her voice to work was even harder than she'd expected. "Yes, you're re-membering right. I'm sorry to bother you, but I wonder if we could talk."

Thea looked her over uncertainly. "If it's about the Center, I'd rather wait until tomor-row. I'll be there from eleven until three."

"It's not about the Center," Jolene said. "At least not directly."

Thea's uncertainty turned to suspicion. "How did you find me here? Did someone at the Center give out my address?"

"No, actually I got it from Mason Black-fox."

"From Mason?"

"Yes, he— He's been a good friend." When Thea made no move to invite her in, she blurted in desperation, "I think you knew my mother."

Confusion clouded her grandmother's eyes. "Your mother?"

"Her name is Margaret. She used to be Margaret Starr."

One hand flew to Thea's throat and her eyes grew round with surprise. "Oh, my. You're Maggie's daughter?"

Jolene couldn't imagine her mother going by a nickname but, then, she wouldn't have believed any of this a few weeks ago. "I am."

"Why didn't you say so before?" Thea motioned Jolene inside. "Well, then, of course. Come in out of the rain. I have a feeling this is going to take a while."

Profoundly relieved, Jolene followed the small woman into a large room dominated by a loom and a half-finished blanket in shades of red, yellow and gray. Against the far wall, baskets tumbled over one another and thin strips of wood and a stack of handles lay on a large workspace. Another blanket hung on the wall, and still another over the arm of a chair.

Jolene turned slowly, taking it all in, trying to get a feel for the woman who lived there. "Mason told me you're a master craftsman. He didn't mention that you also weave blankets."

"I do many things. Come. Sit. Tell me about Maggie. How is she?"

"She's fine." Jolene sat and waited to drop her bombshell until Thea was comfortable. "My mother tells me my father was your son, Billy."

CHAPTER TWENTY-TWO

THEA'S EXPRESSION changed dramatically at that news. Suspicion, confusion and hope all mingled together on her face. "Billy's child? But that's impossible. He's been gone—"

"For thirty years. I know." Jolene tried to smile, but her lips felt like cold lumps of clay. "Apparently, my mother was pregnant when Billy was killed in Vietnam."

Thea closed her eyes. "And she never told me?"

"She never told me, either. I only recently found out."

"But how can that be?"

"She was...I mean, she thought...it's a long story. I didn't know who you were when I met you at the Center. Mason didn't tell me until later."

"Mason knows who you are?"

"Yes.

"I see. And this is true, what you say? You're really my granddaughter?"

"According to my mother. I believe her."

Thea leaned forward and studied Jolene for so long, she had to grip the armrests to keep from fidgeting. "There is a lot of your mother in you," Thea said after what seemed like hours. "But I see my son, too—in your eyes, your chin, even the tilt of your head as you look at me." Her eyes brimmed with tears and she sat back in her chair with a sigh. "Why did she tell you after all this time? If she's kept it a secret for thirty years, why now?"

"She probably wouldn't have if I hadn't stumbled across an old photograph of her with Billy while I was working on a case."

"A case?"

"I'm a police officer."

"And you found a photograph of Billy and Maggie together? After all this time?"

"It was at Mason's house. That's how we met. Not because of the picture, really. I was there for another reason."

"I see."

"I wasn't even on a case," Jolene said,

suddenly worried that she might have added to the doubts about Mason. "I was giving Debra a lift home. After a party."

Thea crossed her legs and set her rocking chair in motion. "You seem very sweet."

Jolene laughed uncertainly. "Thanks, but sweet isn't a word most people use with me. Comes from working on the narcotics squad for too long, I guess."

"A police officer. Isn't that something. Billy would have liked that."

The quick rush of pleasure she felt surprised Jolene. "Would he?"

"He was a warrior, that son of mine. Always wanting to right some wrong or protect someone who needed help. An *Aniwayha* born to the *Anisahoni*. His father never understood, and neither did his brothers. It wasn't easy on him, I can tell you that." She was silent for a moment. "Why didn't your mother tell you about Billy? Was she ashamed?"

Jolene shook her head quickly. "She says she wasn't, and again, I believe her. She says she loved Billy, but she was confused and frightened after he died. And worried her parents wouldn't accept me."

Thea stopped rocking. "They always had trouble accepting the marriage. It was hard on Maggie right from the beginning."

"But that doesn't excuse her for hiding the truth from me all my life."

"My son adored your mother and the rest of us adored her, as well. If she kept a secret from you, she must have thought she had a reason."

"What reason can there be for lying?"

"It's easy to second-guess, but you'll never know if her choice was right or wrong, will you? Your life is what it is, and you are who you are because of that choice."

"You make it sound so simple."

"But it is. You can accept it or not, that's up to you. You can make this difficult and move through your life with anger and hostility toward your parents, or you can accept what happened and love them. It won't change anything except you."

The slight reprimand surprised her, but in some strange way she didn't understand, it made her feel as if she belonged to this small woman with the intelligent eyes. "You're probably right. I just don't know if I'm ready—"

"What will it take to make you ready?" When Jolene didn't answer, her grandmother nodded knowingly. "It's in your hands, child. If you had known sooner, you might not be who you are right now. And the important thing is that you've found us and you've come home. You're here when you were meant to be here, so let's not waste time with anger."

If only it were that easy.

Thea's gaze roamed Jolene's face again, and a tiny smile curved her lips. "I can see the ancestors in your face. The shape of your eyes. Your nose." Her smile grew big and warmth filled her eyes. "Your uncles will be so happy to meet you. And so will your cousins."

Instinctively, Jolene pulled back from the thought of a large extended family. But withdrawing into herself hadn't made her life a bed of roses so far. Even with issues and problems, her life seemed more full and interesting for having Mason and Debra in it. Opening the door to the rest of her family might enrich it even more.

"How many are there?"

"Two uncles. Ten…no, nine cousins. And you."

Thea's voice was so kind, Jolene's fear began to melt away. "Tell me about them?"

"About your uncles?"

She nodded, surprised at how shy she felt. "About my uncles. My cousins." She took another deep breath. "But mostly about my father."

Thea settled back with a satisfied smile and began to speak. And Jolene, with tears in her eyes, curled into her chair to listen.

AT A LITTLE AFTER TEN, Jolene waved at Thea on the front porch and climbed into the cab at the curb. She was worn-out emotionally and physically, exhausted from the hours of laughing and crying, taking in everything her grandmother had told her, and the shock of recognition she'd felt when she'd looked at Thea's small collection of photographs. For the first time in weeks, she knew everything was going to be all right.

She leaned her head against the backseat and closed her eyes. The wound on her leg was beginning to throb and her arm ached, and the only thing she wanted now was to go home, climb into bed and spend some time processing everything she'd learned today.

Before the cab had gone even a mile, her cell phone rang. She dug it from her pocket, checked the caller ID and flipped it open. "What's up, Ry?"

"We got him."

"Got who?"

"Red. Couple of patrol officers spotted him three blocks from the GemCrest Toys warehouse. I'm going to talk to him in a few minutes. Thought maybe you'd like to come for the party."

Suddenly awake, Jolene sat upright. "Give me ten minutes, and save me a party hat."

She made it in nine and found Ryan talking to a couple of uniformed officers she didn't recognize in the windowless corridor that separated the holding cells from the interrogation rooms.

He glanced up at the sound of her hurried footsteps and grinned. "That was quick."

"I was already in a cab. What's going on?"

"I haven't talked to him yet, but I was just about to. You want to watch?"

"Watch? No. I want to talk to him."

"Captain Eisley's not going to go for that and you know it. You're not on active duty."

"But this is my case."

"It's *our* case, Jo, and I probably shouldn't even let you be here. Give me a break, okay? Take what I can give you."

Biting back her objections, she gave a crisp nod and slipped into the small, dark observation room.

Red was already in the interrogation room sitting in front of a long, narrow table, head bent, eyes downcast. He was still wearing the clothes Jolene had seen him in the other day, and she swore she could actually smell the body odor through the two-way mirror separating them. An armed guard stood in the corner, unobtrusive and almost invisible, there only to step in if things got out of hand.

Naomi Beck's careworn face flashed into her mind, and Jolene wondered how someone like Russell Beck could go from a home with every advantage to this, while someone like Mason could begin life with nothing and become a productive, useful member of society. Was it just a crapshoot? She'd probably never know.

The door to the interrogation room opened and Ryan, wearing a dour expression, swaggered inside. He carried a thick file folder and everything from his posture to the look on his face said "Don't mess with me."

Red's head popped up when he heard the door open. He took one look at Ryan and tried to stand. "Hey, man, what the hell? Why'd those idiots bring me in here? I haven't done anything."

The armed guard stepped forward and pressed Red back into his seat. With a gesture that Jolene knew was deliberately casual, Ryan tossed the folder onto the desk. "You know, Red, I was about to ask you the same question. What the hell? What are you doing attacking police officers? Don't you know that can get a guy into a lot of trouble?"

"Attack—? Who, me?" Red did his best to look outraged and innocent. "You've got the wrong guy. I never attacked anybody."

"Yeah? Well I think you did, and my partner—" Ryan perched on one corner of the table and jerked his head toward the mirror "—she thinks you did, too. But maybe you're just too high to remember."

Red's eyes—the only thing his beard didn't cover—flashed toward the mirror. "She's in there watching us?"

"Got the cast on her arm and everything. She'd really rather be in here talking to you."

That was an understatement. Jolene leaned in close to the speaker, straining to hear every word.

"What's that," Red asked. "Some kind of threat?"

Ryan laughed. "Just a statement of fact, buddy. I have to tell you, my partner's tough. She's real tough. Shoving her off those stairs was a mistake."

Red sank back in his chair and stared into Ryan's eyes. "And I told you, you're talking to the wrong guy."

"She can ID you if we need her to." Ryan leaned forward, lowering his voice so Jolene had trouble hearing him. "The sad part of it is, we were trying to help you. My partner had this idea that you were in some kind of trouble. She thought maybe you knew something about Zika and his boys that had you worried. But I don't know what to tell you now. It's hard to work up enthusiasm for helping out somebody who shoves you off a flight of stairs and breaks your arm."

"I never shoved anybody off any stairs,"

Red repeated. "I haven't seen you *or* her in weeks."

"Well, like I said, maybe you're just too high to remember."

"I don't get high."

"No?" Ryan glanced amused at the mirror and shrugged. "Well, we'll find out. Maybe I'm wrong. So like I said, Red, we've been looking for you for a while. Ever since the night Raoul Zika was supposed to move that drug shipment. Remember that?"

Red shook his head. "I don't know what you're talking about."

"You've got a real short memory, don't you? I've heard that drugs can do that to a guy. Let me refresh it. April fourteenth. It was a Friday night. The night before you wiped out your mother's checking account and disappeared with all her money. Ring any bells?"

"I never disappeared. I've been around this whole time."

"You have?"

"I have."

"You're not hiding from Zika and his goons?"

"No."

Jolene ground her teeth in frustration. Could she make a difference if she were in there? Probably not. Ryan was good at this. He knew how to do his job. But the waiting was driving her crazy.

"Sorry. My mistake." Ryan stood and started toward the door. "I ran into a couple of Zika's guys the other day. They were asking about you. I'll just let them know you're here. Maybe they can swing by and pick you up when we let you go."

Red snorted and tried to look unconcerned. "You're going to call Zika? Get real, Detective Fielding. You won't give me up, and we both know it."

"Won't I? Far as I know, Raoul Zika and his boys are just concerned members of society. No reason not to let them know their buddy's been found, is there? They seemed real worried."

Red shifted his weight in his chair. "Raoul Zika's no friend of mine, and neither is anybody who works for him."

"Then why are they looking for you?"

"You'd have to ask them."

"I can do that," Ryan said with a shrug. "Not a problem. Maybe I'll bring them in right now. It'll be easier to get the story when you're all together."

For the first time, uncertainty crossed Red's face, and Jolene felt a surge of anticipation.

"You're going to bring them in here? Now?"

"Sure. Unless you can give me a good reason not to."

Red's eyes darted around the room, from the mirror to Ryan's face, to the guard and back again. "If I tell you what I know," he bargained, "will you reduce the charges on the assaulting an officer thing?"

Ryan's expression didn't change, but Jolene knew he was elated. "I'll see what we can do. No promises."

"And those other charges—the possession ones. Can we still work on those?"

Slowly, Ryan closed the door and returned to the table. "Well, now, that's going to depend on what you give us. Why don't you start at the beginning?"

Red didn't speak for a long time. Long enough to make perspiration snake down Jolene's back. Just when she thought Red had changed his mind, he started to talk. "I

can give you Zika for murder," Red said, his
eyes locked on Ryan's, "but only if you
promise to protect me."

CHAPTER TWENTY-THREE

JUST AFTER MIDNIGHT, Jolene used the spare key her parents kept hidden for her use and Trevor's, and let herself into the house. All the lights were out, and she was afraid she might worry them, but they always seemed to know when one of their children was in the house.

Yawning, she climbed the stairs toward their bedroom.

She'd grown up with two loving parents who'd given her everything a child could ever want. She'd been showered with love and attention. They'd met every physical need she'd ever had, and they'd provided far more of the nonessentials than many parents were able to, but still there'd been an emptiness inside. An uncertainty that Jolene had never completely understood, but one, she saw now, that had affected every aspect of her life.

The blame she'd wanted to heap upon her parents had disappeared in the course of the evening, and though part of her still wanted to cling to her outrage, she knew Thea was right. She would only hurt herself if she did, just as Mason had all these years.

Outside her parents bedroom, she paused. As she had so many nights as a little girl, she put her ear to the door and listened for their voices. But except for the rhythmic sound of her father's snoring, the room was silent.

Quickly, before she could change her mind, she knocked and turned the knob. "Mom? Dad? Can I come in for a minute?"

"Jolene?" Her mother's sleepy voice floated out of the darkness. "What is it, honey? Is something wrong?"

"No. Everything's fine. I just need to talk to you."

Sheets rustled as her mother sat up and turned on her bedside lamp. The floral scent of her mother's night cream filled the room. "What is it, sweet pea?"

There would be no recriminations, Jolene realized with relief. In spite of everything she'd said, and the anger she'd poured out on them, her parents had just been waiting for her to get her act together and come home. Was that a special skill, a gene some people were born with, or could anyone learn how to love so unconditionally?

Her father grunted and rolled onto his side. Jolene smiled. Even in sleep, he still had that uncanny ability to remain focused on his task.

Strangely nervous, Jolene moved to the bed and sat at her mother's feet. This, too, was an old ritual. She'd sat this way many nights after dates in high school or outings with friends, and her mother had always listened, eager to share whatever Jolene wanted to talk about.

Her eyes blurred softly and her throat tightened with emotion. "I thought you should know, I just came from Thea's."

Her mother's worry turned to fear in a heartbeat. "Oh?"

Jolene couldn't bear to see her mother frightened, so she reached for her hand. "She'd like to see you again."

Margaret pulled back slightly. Without makeup she looked tired, and smaller than usual. "Is she mad at me?"

"No. She misses you. She'd like to meet Dad, too."

Tears fell to Margaret's cheeks. "After everything I've done?"

"What did you do, Mom? You gave her a granddaughter, and you loved and protected me. Thea seems more interested in the future than the past."

With a sniff, Margaret reached for a tissue on the nightstand. "That sounds like Thea."

Jolene gave her mother's hand a squeeze. It felt tiny in hers, like the delicate wing of a bird. "I think I'm going to be okay. I think *we* are going to be okay."

"Oh, thank God." Margaret's free hand fluttered in Jolene's and her eyes closed in relief. "I'm so sorry, honey. I never meant to hurt you."

"I know, Mom. I know." There were so many things they needed to talk about, but Jolene was too tired and emotionally drained to begin, and her mother deserved time to process this new development.

Wiping tears away with the back of her hand, she leaned in to kiss her mother's cheek. "It's going to be okay, Mom. I'm going to spend the night and we can talk in the morning, okay?"

Working through tough issues together

was what families were for. Jolene knew that. She'd always known it, but she'd lost it somewhere along the way. How odd that it took someone like Mason—someone with no real experience in a family—to bring that lesson home to her again.

She closed her parents' door behind her and walked softly down the hall toward her childhood bedroom, but the comparisons between her life and her mother's raced through her head with every step. The past month had been one of the most painful of her life, and she was almost certain it ranked right up there for her mother. Through it all, her father had been there, a solid, steady strength for her mother to lean on. It wasn't a one-sided relationship either. Jolene could have cited half a dozen times when her mother had been the strong one. *That's* what families were for.

She sat for about two minutes on the foot of her bed before the full impact of her decision to leave Mason's hit her. When it did, she was off the bed like a shot and knocking on her parents' door.

"Mom?" she said as she inched the door open again. "I've got to go."

"What? Now? Is it work?"

"No. It's something better. Would it be okay if I came back for dinner tomorrow night? And could I bring a couple of friends along?"

"Friends?" Her mother sat upright and Jolene could almost see the delight on her face. "Anyone special?"

"Yeah. He is," she said. "And so's his daughter. I hope you get a chance to find out just how special."

IT WAS ONE O'CLOCK in the morning when Jolene pulled into the parking lot of the apartment complex and drove slowly past Mason's building. To her surprise, his lights were still on, and she wondered if he was having as much trouble settling down as she was.

Her heart jumped into her throat at the thought of facing him, but if she didn't talk to him now, she might lose her nerve. Now that she knew what she wanted for the rest of her life, she wanted forever to begin immediately. But that didn't stop her hands from growing clammy as she slowly climbed the stairs to his door.

She knocked softly so she wouldn't wake Debra and chewed the corner of her lip as she heard his footsteps coming. When she saw his shadow through the window, her courage nearly failed her.

The door opened and he stood there, framed by the light. His broad shoulders and shaggy hair made her heart pound. The look in his eyes when he realized who she was made her weak in the knees. "Jolene? What's wrong?"

"Nothing. I just need to talk to you."

He stepped aside to let her enter, and she breathed in his scent as she walked through the door. She'd worked so hard to become a strong, self-reliant woman. Yes, she could make it through this life alone. But she didn't want to.

He looked as if he wanted to scoop her up in his arms, but Jolene could tell he was holding himself back. "I just came from my mother's house," she said. "We're going to be okay."

"I'm glad."

"I saw Thea, too. Earlier. You were right, you know. My big problem was that I didn't know what to do with two families. It seems kind of silly, actually."

"When something hurts, we react. It's human nature."

"I was going to stay at my parents' house tonight, but I wanted to share what happened today." How could opening her heart to someone be more frightening than working the beat? She wished he'd say or do something to let her know what he was feeling, but he was still waiting for her. "I need to share it with you. This is all new territory to me, and I'm afraid I'm not negotiating it very well."

The light that flickered in Mason's eyes made her warm all over. "You seem to be doing just fine."

"Apparently, I told you the other night that it would be easy to fall in love with you. I was pretty out of it at the time, so I need you to know I feel the same way when I'm all here."

Mason moved closer and trailed his fingers along her shoulders, gently at first, then applying more pressure and massaging away the tension. "I meant what I said, too. Falling in love with you wouldn't be difficult." He leaned his forehead against her cheek and whispered, "I don't know if you've noticed, but I'm not perfect, either. We're both going to have to work at this."

She searched his face, surprised by how familiar it had become to her in just a few weeks. Excitement fluttered low in her belly, but with Debra in the next room she couldn't let it overwhelm her. She slid her good arm around his neck and leaned up to kiss him. "As long as you're patient with me when I stumble."

"I think I can handle that." He caught her bottom lip with his teeth and nipped it lightly, then trailed kisses along her throat to the pulse point in her neck. He kissed her gently, then suckled the skin while the fingers of one hand worked to release the buttons on her blouse. She wanted to stop him. She didn't want to stop him, but Debra...

Nudging the soft cotton aside, he moved his mouth lower. His hands cupped her breasts, bare now except for the sheer fabric of her bra. Desire found every female part of her body and set her on fire. She couldn't catch her breath.

He slid his fingers beneath her bra and found tender flesh and nipples grown agonizingly sensitive since their first kiss. He lowered her onto the couch and pressed one thigh between her legs as he worked magic on her mouth, her neck, her breasts, her mind.

She arched against him, needing more. But they couldn't. Somehow she managed to catch her breath long enough to remind him. "Debra."

He lowered his head to her breast and pulled her nipple into his mouth, scorching her.

"Debra," she gasped again, wishing she could make him understand. She wanted everything he was doing and much, much more, but they couldn't risk this. "Mason, we can't—"

"Debra's spending the night with Ike and Barbara," he said with a smile that made her shiver.

"She's gone."

"All night." He kissed her again, quickly. "Alex called last night. She's going to have another baby, and Debra has decided to live with me forever."

"Is she serious?"

"For today." Mason grinned and nuzzled

her earlobe. "I think she and I are going to be okay, too. Which just leaves us."

Jolene slid her hands beneath Mason's soft, faded T-shirt and traced the muscles in his back with her fingertips. She moved her hands to his chest and slid them slowly down to his belt buckle. "Us?"

To her surprise, he stopped her before she could unfasten his belt. "What do you think?" he asked, sliding his arms around her waist. "Do the two of us stand a chance?"

"I can't cook."

"I can't work a set of handcuffs."

She laughed and leaned her cheek against his chest. "It's never going to be just the two of us, Mason. It's going to be your family and mine, Debra and my career…"

"I can handle it, can you?"

She pulled away so she could see him. "I'd sure like to try."

As he bent to kiss her again, Jolene thought about how a life with Mason would be filled with steel-toed boots and meat loaf, homework and handcuffs. Just the way she wanted it.

* * * *

Don't miss the next story in the COUNT ON A COP *series.* Son of Texas *by Linda Warren is available in September 2007.*

MILLS & BOON
Special Edition

On sale 15th June 2007

THE WYOMING KID
by Debbie Macomber

Handsome Lonnie Ellison is used to women throwing
themselves at him. So teacher Joy Fuller's lack of interest
is infuriating…and very appealing!

THE RELUCTANT CINDERELLA
by Christine Rimmer

Megan Schumacher and Greg Banning spent *a lot* of
time together. He was handsome, she was sexy and gossip
was rife. Could this end happily?

PRINCESS IN DISGUISE
by Lilian Darcy

Princess Misha was escaping for a bit in the Australian
Outback. Brant Smith thought she had been sent to him as
a possible wife! Had fate lent love a helping hand?